SHIRLEY JUMP

The Bridesmaid and the Billionaire

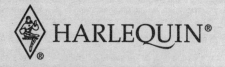

TORONTO • NEW YORK • LONDON
AMSTERDAM • PARIS • SYDNEY • HAMBURG
STOCKHOLM • ATHENS • TOKYO • MILAN • MADRID
PRAGUE • WARSAW • BUDAPEST • AUCKLAND

If you purchased this book without a cover you should be aware that this book is stolen property. It was reported as "unsold and destroyed" to the publisher, and neither the author nor the publisher has received any payment for this "stripped book."

For Sherri, my own maid of honor and best friend, even though she got the part of the narrator in the fourth-grade play. The best part about having her as a best friend is we're never too grown up to have fun.

Recycling programs
for this product may
not exist in your area.

ISBN-13: 978-0-373-17570-3
ISBN-10:   0-373-17570-1

THE BRIDESMAID AND THE BILLIONAIRE

First North American Publication 2009.

Copyright © 2008 by Shirley Kawa-Jump, LLC.

All rights reserved. Except for use in any review, the reproduction or utilization of this work in whole or in part in any form by any electronic, mechanical or other means, now known or hereafter invented, including xerography, photocopying and recording, or in any information storage or retrieval system, is forbidden without the written permission of the publisher, Harlequin Enterprises Limited, 225 Duncan Mill Road, Don Mills, Ontario, Canada M3B 3K9.

This is a work of fiction. Names, characters, places and incidents are either the product of the author's imagination or are used fictitiously, and any resemblance to actual persons, living or dead, business establishments, events or locales is entirely coincidental.

This edition published by arrangement with Harlequin Books S.A.

® and TM are trademarks of the publisher. Trademarks indicated with ® are registered in the United States Patent and Trademark Office, the Canadian Trade Marks Office and in other countries.

www.eHarlequin.com

Printed in U.S.A.

It's
Harlequin's 60th anniversary
this year!

**Harlequin Romance is going to shower you with...
diamond proposals and dazzling weddings,
sparkling brides and gorgeous grooms!**

The Australian's Society Bride
by Margaret Way

Her Valentine Blind Date
by Raye Morgan

The Royal Marriage Arrangement
by Rebecca Winters

Two Little Miracles
by Caroline Anderson

Manhattan Boss, Diamond Proposal
by Trish Wylie

The Bridesmaid and the Billionaire
by Shirley Jump

Whether it's the stunning solitaire ring
that he's offering, the beautiful white dress she's wearing
or the loving vows between them, these stories
will bring a touch of sparkle to your life....

Dear Reader,

Sixty years! What an amazing milestone for Harlequin to have reached! And for me, as an author, to be a part of such an exciting year is so much fun!

I think of the first Harlequin romances I read, back when I was a teenager, and how much I loved those books. I fell in love with the genre, and though I didn't know it at the time, began to find my niche as a writer. These books opened up a huge world to me of strong women and romantic men.

In *The Bridesmaid and the Billionaire*, I've brought one of my favorite kinds of heroes—the wealthy, troubled man—together with a quirky heroine, and some of my absolutely favorite secondary characters: dogs. Anyone who regularly reads my blog (www.shirleyjump.blogspot.com) knows about my new little Havanese puppy, Sophie, and her adventures with my other two dogs. I had a lot of fun writing this book, and introducing some canine characters with personalities all their own!

I hope you enjoy this book, and thank you for being a regular reader of mine, and of Harlequin Romance®. Please write to me, either through my Web site, www.shirleyjump.com, or at Shirley Jump, P.O. Box 5126, Fort Wayne, Indiana 46895, and tell me about your favorite Harlequin Romance® novel. Who knows? Maybe we've got a favorite book in common!

Happy reading,

Shirley

New York Times bestselling author **Shirley Jump** didn't have the willpower to diet, nor the talent to master under-eye concealer, so she bowed out of a career in television and opted instead for a career where she could be paid to eat at her desk—writing. At first, seeking revenge on her children for their grocery-store tantrums, she sold embarrassing essays about them to anthologies. However it wasn't enough to feed her growing addiction to writing funny. So she turned to the world of romance novels, where messes are (usually) cleaned up before The End. In the worlds Shirley gets to create and control, the children listen to their parents, the husbands always remember holidays and the housework is magically done by elves. Though she's thrilled to see her books in stores around the world, Shirley mostly writes because it gives her an excuse to avoid cleaning the toilets and helps feed her shoe habit. To learn more, visit her Web site at www.shirleyjump.com.

Praise for Shirley Jump

"Shirley Jump's *Miracle on Christmas Eve* has a solid plot and involving conflict, and the characters are wonderful."
—*Romantic Times BOOKreviews*

About *Sweetheart Lost and Found*

"This tale of rekindled love is right on target:
a delightful start to this uplifting, marriage-orientated series
[THE WEDDING PLANNERS]."
—*LibraryJournal.com*

About *New York Times* bestselling anthology
Sugar and Spice

"Jump's office romance gives the collection a kick,
with fiery writing."
—*PublishersWeekly.com*

DIAMOND BRIDES

Share your dream wedding proposal
and you could win a stunning diamond necklace!

For more information
visit www.DiamondBridesProposal.com.

CHAPTER ONE

KANE Lennox's bare feet sank into the new spring grass, his toes disappearing between the thick green blades like shy mice. He'd slept on mattresses that cost as much as a small sedan, walked on carpet that had been hand loomed in the Orient, and worn shoes made to order specifically for his feet by a cobbler in Italy. But those experiences paled in comparison to this one. Comfort slid through his veins, washing over him in a wave, lapping at the stress that normally constricted his heart, easing the emotion's death grip on his arteries.

He halted midstep, tossing the conundrum around in his mind. How could something so simple, so basic, as walking barefoot on grass, feel so wonderful?

"What on earth do you think you're doing?"

Kane whirled around at the sound of the woman's voice. Tall and thin, her blond hair hanging in a long straight curtain to her waist, she stood with tight fists propped on her hips. Her features were delicate, classic, with wide green eyes and lush dark pink lips, but right now her face had been transformed by a mask of confusion and annoyance. In one hand she held a cell phone, her thumb over the send button, 9-1-1 just a push away.

Not that he could blame her. Even he had to admit what he was doing looked…odd. Out of place. Kane put up both hands. The "See, I'm okay, not carrying any lethal weapons" posture. "There's a perfectly logical explanation for my behavior," he said. "And my presence."

She raised a dubious brow, but looked a bit worried, even apprehensive. "A total stranger. Barefoot. On my sister's lawn. In the middle of the day. Uh-huh. I'm sure there's a logical explanation for *that*." She turned, casting a hand over her eyes, shading them from the sun. "Either there's some cameraman waiting to jump out of the shrubbery with a 'Surprise, you're on *Candid Camera*' announcement, or you're here on some loony-bin field trip."

He laughed. "I assure you, I'm not crazy."

Though the last few weeks had driven him nearly to insanity. Which had pushed him to this point. To the small town of Chapel Ridge, in the middle of Indiana. To—

Being barefoot on, as she had said, her sister's lawn in the middle of a bright April day. Okay, so it was mildly crazy.

"That leaves the *Candid Camera* option, which I'm definitely not in the mood for, or…trespassing." She held up the phone like a barrier against a vampire. "Either way, I'm calling the cops."

"Wait." He took a step forward, thought better of it and backed up. As his gaze swept over her a second time, he realized she looked familiar, and now knew why. "You must be…" He racked his brain. Usually he was so good at names. But this time, he couldn't come up with hers. "The sister of the bride. Jackie's sister."

"I get it. You're a detective who does his best thinking in his bare feet, is that it?" She gave him a sardonic grin. "Must have been tough, putting all the puzzle pieces together, what with the Congratulations Jackie and Paul sign out front, the paper wedding bells hanging on the mailbox. Oh, and the happiness emanating from the house like cheap perfume." She paused midtirade. "Wait. How do you know who *I* am?"

Kane gave her an assessing glance, avoiding the question. "What's made you so disagreeable?"

She sighed and lowered the phone. "I've had a rough day. A rough life and—" She cut herself off again. "How do you *do* that? I'm not telling you a single thing about me."

"Listen, I'll just get out of here and leave you to your day. I've clearly come at a bad time." He bent over, picked up his designer Italian leather dress shoes and started to leave.

"Wait." She let out a gust.

He turned back and for a second, Kane swore he heard a spark of himself—of the last few months, the days that had driven him to this town, to this crazy idea—in that sound. Then, just as quickly, it was gone, and the spark of distrust had returned.

"You still haven't told me why you're barefoot on the lawn in the middle of the day."

Kane's jaw hardened. "We're back to that again?"

"When did we ever leave that topic?" She parked her fists back on her hips, the cell phone dangling between two fingers.

Telling her why he was here, and what he was doing, involved getting into far too many personal details. If he started opening up about his problems, he'd have all of Chapel Ridge—all 4,910 residents, as it were—knowing his identity, and there'd go his plan to enjoy some much-needed R & R.

He had no intentions of telling anyone anything. Particularly Jackie's sister.

Susannah Wilson. That was her name. Suzie-Q, Paul called her, like the packaged dessert.

Before she could question him further, he headed over to his little blue rental car, a cheap American model, light-years away from the silver convertible Bentley Azure he usually drove. The rental was nondescript, plain. Like something anyone else in the world would be driving. And perfect.

Susannah followed him. Not one to give up easily, that was clear. "You still didn't answer my question. Who are you? And why are you here?"

"That's two questions. And I don't have to tell you anything, either. It's a free country."

He could almost hear her internal scream of frustration. Oh, this was going to be fun.

She scowled. "Trespassing is a crime, you know."

He grinned. When he'd booked this trip, he'd had no idea there'd be a fringe benefit of this little fireball. "Only if you're not invited. And *I* was invited." He paused a beat, watching her eyes widen in surprise at the word *invited*, waiting to deliver the last punch of surprise. "I'm the best man, after all."

"You have the worst taste in friends."

Paul Hurst, Jackie's fiancé, laughed. "Suzie-Q, you need to give Kane the benefit of the doubt. He's not so bad. And he had his reasons for what he was doing, I'm sure."

"Where did you meet him anyway? Prison?"

"College. He had the room next door to mine, and we had a few classes together. And he's—" Paul cut himself off. "He's a good guy. Just trust me on that."

Susannah got to her feet, gathering the mess of dishes on the coffee table. The collection of plates and glasses had grown over the day, multiplying like bunnies in her absence. Jackie and Paul didn't move from their positions in the living room of the old Victorian-style house. Paul had his feet up on the scarred maple coffee table—a garage sale find of Susannah's from last summer—and Jackie was curled up beside him, the remote control in her hands. Across the room, a detective show played on the big-screen TV, an early wedding gift from Susannah and the brides-maids, who had chipped in on the electronic extravaganza. "The last time I trusted you, you stole my sister's heart."

Paul laughed. He wrapped an arm around Jackie and drew her to him. The leather sofa, a replacement for the plaid one that had sat in this room for nearly twenty years, creaked beneath his weight. "Just think of it as gaining a brother."

Jackie leaned into the brown-haired man she had dated for the better part of three years and gave him a kiss on the cheek. "A very handsome brother."

Susannah grinned. "Santa must not have heard me when I said I wanted a *pony*."

She headed out of the room, the dishes in her hands, and loaded them into the sink. She ran hot water over them, added dish soap, then started washing. She had stood at this sink for nearly all her life, looked out this same window at the same yard, washing dishes ever since she'd been old enough to stand on the small wooden stepstool and reach into the deep-bottomed stainless steel sink. Back then, she'd washed while her mother dried, the two of them fall-ing into a natural rhythm, working along with the radio in the background, and the sunny yellow kitchen seemed to beam back the sunshine in her mother's voice.

But those days were gone, the radio had broken years ago, and the kitchen's paint had faded. And now the dishes had become a chore.

"You don't have to do that," Jackie said. She leaned against the refrigerator, filing her nails with an emery board. "If you let them sit—"

"They won't break," Jackie cut in. "Leave the dishes for later. Or even better, don't do them at all."

If Susannah didn't do them, they'd never get done. Neither Jackie nor Paul was much for housework, despite their protests to the contrary. In exchange for living with the two of them for a nominal rent to help pay down the mortgage, Susannah had agreed to do the majority of the housework and even though the deal had worked out so that she ended up doing all the chores, most days the arrangement suited her just fine. It helped her save money, which went to her ultimate goal.

Freedom.

One week. Just one more week, and she'd be out of here. Out of this house. Out of this town. On her way to the life she had dreamed of for so long it seemed like she had been born with the dream. Susannah's gaze drifted to the stained-glass Eiffel Tower hanging in the kitchen window. Gold and orange glints bounced off the countertops as the sun's afternoon's rays streamed through the tiny glass shards.

I've never been here, her mother had said, that last Christmas when she'd given Susannah the small reproduction of Paris's famous landmark, *but I hope someday you can go, sweet Susannah. See the world I never got to see.*

Susannah would. No matter what it took.

"I'll just get these few before I go to work," Susannah said.

"But you just got home. I thought you were done for the day."

"I had a couple late appointments. Every appointment is another dollar, you know." She gave Jackie a smile.

"You work too hard." Jackie held her hands out, checked all ten fingers, deemed them perfect and tucked the file into her back pocket.

"All for the ultimate goal, sis. All for the ultimate goal."

"A discreet way of saying you hate living with us." Jackie laughed, showing Susannah no offense was taken, then gave her sister a quick hug. "Oh, when you go out, do you mind doing me a favor?"

"Sure."

"Can you stop by and pick up the centerpieces? I have a fitting tonight and then…"

"The party."

The bachelorette party. The same one that Susannah had planned, as maid of honor, but wasn't attending. She'd never known Jackie's friends very well, and as the date had approached, felt herself less and less inclined to spend the evening with the other bridesmaids. Women who had always been Jackie's friends and included Susannah only as an afterthought, like adding one more fern to an already perfect floral arrangement.

"You can still come. You are one of the bridesmaids, after all. The bachelorette party is one of the perks." Jackie grinned.

"I'm cool, Jackie. Really." She ran the sponge over a plate, scrubbing at the center until the stoneware gleamed. "I'm not much for parties anyway."

"You're just avoiding, like you always do."

"No, I'm not. I have to work."

Jackie sighed but let the subject drop. She placed a hand on Susannah's shoulder. "I appreciate you picking the centerpieces up. You're really saving me. Again."

Not that Susannah had the time. She had three dogs to bathe tonight, and a million errands of her own. "What about Paul?"

"Nothing against my future husband, but I don't think he'd know a centerpiece from a centrifuge." She laughed.

Susannah increased the water temperature, filling a casserole dish that had been used for nachos or cheese dip, or something equally hardened and stubborn about giving up its baked-on grip. "When were you planning on assembling them?"

"Assembling them?" Jackie paused, then smacked her temples. "Damn. I totally forgot about that part. Maybe tomorrow afternoon." She thought a second. "No, wait. That's the meeting with the minister to go over the rest of the ceremony details. Umm…tomorrow night? No, not then, either. Paul and I have plans with the Fitzgeralds. Remember them? They used to be Mom and Dad's friends. I don't know how long we'll be at their house. You know how they can talk. And then on Thursday night we have the reh—"

"Basically, you have a million other things to do," Susannah finished.

As usual. Jackie's list was filled with social engagements and outings and very few responsibilities. At twenty-six, Susannah was four years older than Jackie and had always run her life down the opposite track. She bit back a breath of annoyance. Soon Jackie would be married, and she'd *have* to be responsible. Because Susannah wouldn't be here anymore to carry the load.

"It's a wonder I have time to go to work with all that, huh?" Jackie said, laughing. "Believe me, if Paul and I didn't need the money, I'd be calling in sick every day. Gosh, how on earth am I ever going to find time to do everything for the wedding? It's like the clock is running out. Jerry said we could set up early at the hotel, because they have nothing else scheduled there this weekend, but I don't even have time to…"

Her voice trailed off and then that hopeful smile took over her face. The one Susannah knew as well as she knew every square inch of this house. Jackie leaned against the counter and met Susannah's gaze. "Hey, what are *you* doing tonight, sis?"

Susannah pulled the drain on the sink. "No way, Jackie. I've got—"

"Please, Suzie-Q. Please?" Jackie put her hands together, and gave Susannah a pleading-puppy-dog look. "Just this one more favor, and then, I swear, I'll never ask for another. I swear."

And Susannah said yes. Just like always.

CHAPTER TWO

KANE could run a multi-billion-dollar, fourth-generation, international gem import company. Negotiate million-dollar deals. Understand the most complicated of financial reports. Surely he could do something as simple as light a fire. The flame on the match met the log, sputtered briefly, then poof, disappeared.

Apparently not.

He'd rented the cabin on the outskirts of town, ordered a quarter-cord of wood, picked up some matches at the store downtown, and thought the whole process would be as simple as striking a match to a box, then holding it against a stick.

Uh…not exactly.

Kane let out a curse as his sixth attempt fizzled and died, then stalked outside. He drew in several deep breaths of fresh, country air. An hour ago, he'd been loving the whole experience. Now he was ready to call his chauffeur, have him hurry the hell out here with the limo and drive him straight to the private Lennox Gem Corporation jet.

No. He'd do this. He *needed* to do this.

He stepped back and appraised the situation with logic, thinking back over movies he'd seen and the books about camping he'd skimmed on the plane when he'd taken this impromptu escape from reality. Too many large, thick logs. Not enough skinny sticks. What he needed was more kindling. Not more thinking.

Kane headed outside, blew some warm air on his cold hands, then started picking up sticks from the ground. As he did, his hands brushed against the bare dirt, pushing soil under his nails when he dug into the earth to loosen a stubborn piece. He pulled his hand back and marveled at the sight of the dirt.

Such a simple thing, and yet, he'd never done this. Never had soil beneath his nails. Never cleaned mud from his uncalloused palms. Kane kneeled down and pressed both hands into the soft dark brown earth, squeezing the thick clumps. A burst of rich, earthy scent filled his nostrils. Then the dirt broke apart, slipping through his fingers and hitting the ground again with a soft patter, like fat raindrops.

Kane chuckled. Imagine that. One of the richest men in the world, amused at something so basic as communing with Mother Nature.

Something shivered the bushes beside him. Kane jerked to attention, grabbing his kindling as he did. He thrust his right hand forward, then realized his sapling ammunition made him about as dangerous as a sunflower. "Who's there?"

Or rather, *what* was there?

When he'd made the decision two days ago to come here for more than just Paul's wedding, he'd done a quick research overview of the location, right down to the last lack of amenities, but hadn't thought to look up "wild indigenous animals." For God's sake, the thing rustling around five feet from him could be a bear.

The rustling grew louder, the leaves shaking like can-can dancers. Kane took a step back. Should he head for the cabin? Stand his ground? He could just see the headline now: Idiot CEO Billionaire Dies: Money No Match For Bear In Woods.

The press would have a field day with that one. He'd be the butt of jokes for generations to come.

Then, out of the woods, a bundle of fur came bounding right for him, and Kane started to turn and run back inside, until he realized the bundle was—

A dog.

The mutt, a small barrel of brown-and-white fur and floppy ears, barked at him, then leapt at his legs, tongue lolling, tail wagging. Oh, God, it was *on* him now. Shedding. Kane had no experience with pets. Not unless he counted the one week his mother thought it would be cute to have a pocket pooch, then changed her mind once she realized live dogs actually peed and pooped—and gave the dog to the maid.

This thing was as friendly as a second-place politician desperate for every last vote. Kane took a step back, hands up, his sticks like finger extensions. "Whoa, there, buddy. Get down. Please."

Undaunted, the dog kept coming, launching himself at Kane in another greeting. Kane reached out a tentative hand, and gave the dog an awkward pat on the head. "There you go. Now go on home."

The dog barked, plopped his butt on the ground and swished a semicircle into the ground with his tail.

"Go home."

The dog's tail widened the dirt semicircle, creating a tiny cloud of dust. He barked disagreement. Stubborn.

"Well, if you won't, I will." Kane pivoted, and headed into the cabin. Before he could shut the door—hands impeded by the load of kindling—the dog was there.

Inside.

With him.

"Oh, no, you don't. Shoo." Kane waved out the door. The dog stayed put, staring at him. Expectant. "Go home."

The dog barked some more. This time it sounded like a feed-me bark. Not that Kane would know, of course, but the way the dog was looking at him, he seemed kind of hungry.

"I don't have any dog food. In fact—"

He didn't have any people food, either. For a man who lived his life by a schedule and a plan, he'd done a pretty lousy job of planning this one.

It was that woman. She'd gotten him all turned around this morning. Set him off-kilter. If he hadn't met her, he wouldn't have forgotten to buy food. Or thoroughly check out his surroundings. Or gather kindling. And then he wouldn't have this…this creature staring at him.

A creature he needed to get rid of. Kane opened the door, but the dog stayed put. Clearly, reasoning with the animal wasn't going to work. The dog wore no collar, so Kane couldn't call his owner. And he certainly couldn't keep the thing here. So he did the only other thing he knew to do—delegate.

He fished his cell phone out of his pocket and punched in the number for the woman who had rented him the cabin. "Mrs. Maxwell, do you own a dog?"

Angela Maxwell, an older woman with gray hair and a friendly smile, and most of all, a tendency not to ask any questions once she had a valid credit-card number in hand, laughed on the other end of the phone. "No, dear, I don't. But there are lots of stray dogs around the cabins. Sometimes they get separated from their owners who are on vacation. And we don't have much of a leash law 'round here. People kind of just let their dogs go, it being a small town and all. Most everybody knows most everybody else's dogs."

"Do you know this one? It's brown and white. Short. Stubborn." Kane glared at the dog. It swished its tail and, he swore, grinned at him.

"Well, no, can't say that I do, but I know who would know. You take that pooch on down to The Sudsy Dog. The owner there, she runs a sort of pet rescue thing. She'll help you out."

"The Sudsy Dog?"

"It's a hot dog wash." Mrs. Maxwell laughed at the pun. "Just off of Main Street. You can't miss it. On the sign you'll see—"

"Let me guess. A hot dog in a tub?"

"You got it. Except, he's really a dachshund. It's the cutest dang sign ever. My Orin painted it himself." Then she hung up.

Kane groaned. He looked down at the dog, who looked back up at him, still wagging. "Looks like we're going for a ride."

That got the dog off his feet. He popped to all fours, tail beating a drum of anticipation against Kane's leg. Kane headed out to his rental car, trying not to cringe at the thought of dog hair all over the leather interior, then opened the door. Before he could say "Lay down on the floor," the dog was sitting right beside the driver's seat.

Looked like he was going to have a new best friend for the next few minutes.

Whether he liked it or not.

Susannah latched the wire crate holding Mrs. Prudhomme's standard poodle, then took off her apron and brushed the bangs off her forehead. "You're looking gorgeous after your beauty treatment, Fancy Pants. Which is more than I can say for me."

The white dog let out a woof, then settled down in the cage to wait for her owner to pick her up. Fancy Pants was in here once every two weeks, and though she barely tolerated the manicures, she enjoyed the grooming process.

Susannah glanced at the Arc de Triomphe poster on her wall. Nine hundred dogs. Three hundred cats. And now she was there—she finally had enough money saved to take that trip. To finally experience a life outside this little town. To put all those years of French classes into practice. To dust off her never-used passport. And see the world.

She traced her finger down the two-dimensional image of the intricate carving of the *Departure of Volunteers on the Arc,* imagining herself in a world so much more glamorous than this one. Heck, working almost anywhere would be more glamorous than doing what she did for a living.

The bell over the door jingled and Susannah let out a sigh. Back to work. And back to reality.

"Take this…this *thing* off my hands. Please."

Susannah turned around and found first, an adorable brown-and-white dog at her feet. Then, a fuming best man behind him. The same man from the morning, only this time he was wearing shoes—and a frown. "You again."

"I could say the same thing. *You* work *here?*"

She nodded, not bothering to correct him and tell him she owned the business. Susannah bent down to scratch the dog behind the ears. He let out a happy groan and pressed himself against her legs, his tail wagging. "Is this your dog?"

"God, no. He's some stray who can't seem to get the hint."

She arched a brow. "Seems to be a lot of those in town lately."

Kane leaned an elbow on the cabinet and gave her a

smirk. When he did, the facial gestured transformed him, taking Kane from ordinary to…

Well, extraordinarily handsome, almost playboy handsome, like something out of a magazine. A quiver ran through Susannah's gut, but she ignored it.

"You aren't talking about me, are you?" he said.

"Not at all." Susannah's voice raised into high and innocent ranges. She straightened, the dog remaining by her side. "So whose dog is this? He looks like a Brittany spaniel, or a Brit mix."

"You tell me. He just showed up at my cabin." Kane thumbed toward the door, in an easterly direction. "I'm staying in one of the Lake Everett cabins."

He was renting one of the rustic cabins? Sure, he was wearing jeans and a T-shirt, but the shirt was as clean as one straight out of the package. And his shoes—

Now that he was wearing them, she noticed he had on expensive dress shoes. Not the kind anyone would wear in the woods, especially not that kind of leather, which looked as soft as kid gloves. A high gloss bounced light off the finish, which sported fine, delicate stitching.

He was too…perfect to be the typical renter who came into town in the summer, stayed a week or two for the fishing, then went back to his normal life. Kane Lennox could have passed for a cover model, one of those men clad in a three-piece suit, hawking expensive cologne or designer watches. Except…

Except for his eyes. His eyes held a summer storm, the dark blues of passing thunderclouds, the depths of unplumbed mysteries. Behind his cobalt gaze, Susannah wondered, was the real Kane Lennox the man in a suit, or the barefoot man she'd met this morning?

"Well, I don't recognize this little guy," she said, bending down to stroke the dog's silky ears, distancing herself from thoughts of his temporary owner, "but I'll put up a notice in my shop."

"Good. I appreciate you doing so." Kane turned on his heel.

"Wait. You're not leaving him here, are you?"

He stopped in the doorway. "Of course. I couldn't possibly be responsible for the caretaking of a dog."

"Why not? Are you allergic?"

"I don't believe so."

That right there. The way he talked. That, too, didn't fit with the image of a cabin renter. Some weekend fisherman, or an avid hunter on a few days' break from the daily grind. Every one of Paul's friends was the typical guy-next-door, the kind that sat at the bar and knocked back a couple of beers, told a bawdy joke or two. This guy…not at all that type. How on earth did he ever become Paul's friend, and not just friend, but *best* friend?

"Do you have two hands?" Susannah asked.

"Yes." He gave her a dubious look.

"Two legs?"

The dubious look narrowed. "Yes."

"Then that, along with this," Susannah grabbed a five-pound bag of dry dog food from the shelf and thrust it into his arms, "is all you need for now. Even though we take great care of our shelter animals here, we first try to find foster families for them."

"Foster families. For dogs."

"Yep. And since this little guy is already attached to you, it should be no sweat for you to take him home. He'll do much better emotionally with you, at your house, than he would stuck in a kennel all day anyway. And really, all you have to do is feed him, walk him and wait until his owner claims him."

He stared at her. "Are you *completely* insane? I am not a dog person."

Again, he had that air about him. Not just out of town, but completely out of her world. Out of her social stratosphere. Clearly, the man came from some money. He had to, given the way he dressed and talked. Why would someone like that want to stay in Chapel Ridge, Indiana, any longer than he had to?

While they'd been debating, the dog had left Susannah's side and was now plopped down beside Kane, his little snout turned up expectantly. "Apparently he disagrees."

"He's a dog, he doesn't know any better." Kane waved in her direction. "*You* are the hot dog wash person. *You* take him."

"No can do. I'm too busy with the wedding plans."

"Last I checked, you weren't the bride."

No, she wasn't. And Susannah had no intentions of becoming a bride anytime soon, that was for sure. A relationship, especially a serious one, would only derail the dream she'd worked so hard to fulfill.

"Let's just say that being a bridesmaid doesn't lessen my level of responsibility," Susannah said with a little laugh.

Kane eyed her with a visual question mark, but didn't press the issue. "He's just a dog. Surely—"

"You can handle it as easily as I." Susannah ran a hand through her hair. She didn't need one more thing on her to-do list. Couldn't the man see that? He may be handsome, but he had an obstinate streak as long as the Mississippi River.

She grabbed a leash and collar from the shelf and handed those to him, too, adding them to the top of the dog food. "You might want to put the leash to use right now."

"What are you talking about?"

"Rover there has some needs to attend to." She pointed at the dog, who was sniffing at the room like a drug addict.

"He can wait."

"Only if you don't mind him messing up your car later."

It took Kane a second, then he made the connection. His face wrinkled in disgust. "Absolutely not." He waved at her. "Well, tell him to go do what he needs to do then."

Susannah laughed. "I can't tell a dog to do anything, at least when it comes to that particular bodily function. But you could try walking him."

"Why? He has four paws of his own."

Susannah rolled her eyes, then took the leash and collar out of Kane's hand, fitted them onto the dog, then handed the other end back to Kane. "Walking the dog is when *you* move your two legs. The dog will get the idea, believe me."

He stared at her, seeming horrified by the entire idea. "What about you?"

"I have other things to do, like my job." She started to walk away.

"Wait!"

Susannah pivoted back. And nearly laughed out loud. Tall, muscular Kane looked lost. "It's a pretty simple concept, Mr. Lennox. Put one foot in front of the other. Rover will follow. And if you go near some grass, his natural instincts will take over." Before he could protest or ask her to do it, she pointed toward the back door of the shop. "There's some grass right in the back parking lot. It'll take five minutes, I swear."

Kane scowled, but did as she said, walking stiffly out the door, with Rover following behind, pausing every half second to sniff. Susannah watched through the window, biting her lip, trying not to laugh. Too loudly.

A few minutes later, Rover was feeling much better and Kane had returned to the shop. "*Now* will you take him?"

"Why? You're doing great. And besides, you're on vacation, right? Staying at a cabin in the woods? Think of him as…a roommate."

Kane scowled. "I don't want, nor do I need, a roommate."

The dog had plastered himself to Kane's leg. Susannah gave him a grin. An SUV pulled into the parking lot, a familiar golden furball in the passenger's seat. Her next appointment. "Seems like you have one, like it or not. Now, unless you want to help me bathe a golden retriever, and deck her out with some bows in her hair, you might want to head on home with your new best friend."

An incredulous look filled Kane's eyes. "Bows? On a dog?"

"She's a girl. She likes to look pretty. Even if doing so leaves me looking like a sopping wet disaster afterwards," Susannah added, brushing a clump of dog hair off her T-shirt. God, she was a mess. She looked about as good as her canine charges—before their baths.

Not that she cared, of course, what Kane Lennox thought about her appearance. It was simply that this man had her feeling off center. She didn't care at all if he found her unappealing because she'd just finished giving a poodle a bath.

Except a part of her did care. And that part was annoyed that she worried whether she had any lipstick left on her mouth. Whether her bangs were askew. Whether she reeked of eau de puppy.

"What if…" He hesitated. "What if I help you with your work? Will you take this—" he shifted his weight to the opposite foot "—this thing off my hands then?"

"*You're* going to help me give a golden retriever a bath?"

He dropped the bag of dog food onto the counter. The spaniel watched the kibble transfer and heaved a sigh of disappointment. "Why are you so surprised by my offer?"

"You don't strike me as the dog-bathing type. Especially considering the way you're reacting to your new best friend here."

Kane's stance straightened, consciously, or maybe unconsciously, putting some distance between himself and the small dog. "I'm simply making a business proposition. Quid pro quo."

Susannah considered the neatly pressed Kane again. She doubted he had any experience with pets. Nary a shred of shampooing or grooming background. Yet, she'd give about anything to see this stiff, uppity stranger covered in soapy bubbles and dog slobber.

She thrust out her hand and when he took hers, a spark traveled up her arm, taking Susannah completely by surprise. Attracted? To him?

She couldn't be. He was not her type. At all. For one, he had that air of uppercrust about him. For another, he was too vague about who he was, where he was from. She liked the men she dated to be open, friendly.

Sort of like a good golden retriever, come to think of it. This man was more of a Lhasa apso, too pretty to be a workhorse. But if Kane was willing to take a little of the burden off her shoulders, who was she to turn him down?

"You've got a deal, Mr. Lennox," Susannah said, attributing her reaction to him as being too tired, too overworked. "I just hope you can keep up your end of the bargain."

A slow grin stole across his face. "If there's one thing I always do, Miss Wilson, it's make sure that the deal is a win-win for me, too."

And as that smile widened, Susannah had to wonder whether she'd just been outwitted—and whether she'd be the real loser in this proposition.

CHAPTER THREE

INSANE.

Kane Lennox never made spur-of-the-moment offers. Every move in his life had an intention, a purpose, a plan behind it. He operated like a Mercedes with a well-tuned engine and a navigational system. No breakdowns, no detours and no surprises.

Then what on earth had made him open up his mouth and actually *volunteer* to bathe a canine? He didn't even like dogs. Or at least, he didn't think he did. He had no experience with canines, so therefore, no opinion one way or another, except he knew he had no time for that stray, and no room in his life for a spaniel. And yet, here he was, elbow-deep in soapy water beside a way-too-friendly golden retriever.

He glanced over at Susannah Wilson, who was cooing to the dog as she sudsed the animal's head, and knew exactly what had possessed him to throw that sentence out there. Her. She'd distracted him nearly from the minute he'd met her. Combined with the day he'd had, the dog and his discomfort at being in a strange town, out of his normal element—

Oh, hell, it was really all the pretty woman. The way she had half her blond locks tucked behind her ear, the other half drifting along her cheek in damp waves. And the way she stared at him like he was some kind of weird stalker come to invade her town with a highly viral disease.

The combination—attraction mixed with distrust—sparked amusement in him, and raised his interest in her to a level unlike anything he'd felt in a long time.

Kane had met hundreds of women over the course of his life. Dated dozens of them. But in the circles he traveled, the women were too perfect, too pampered. Susannah Wilson, on the other hand, had a less finished edge to her, like a diamond that had yet to be cut and polished. She was…

Unique.

Intriguing. Very intriguing.

"Hey, I thought you were here to help. That means holding her steady," Susannah said.

"Easier said than done," Kane grumbled. "This dog is as slippery as an eel in an oil vat."

Susannah chuckled, then tightened the rainbow paw-printed lead attached from the top of the deep stainless steel tub to the dog's neck, which shortened the dog's roaming room. "Didn't you ever have a pet?"

"No, never."

"Not so much as a gerbil?"

"No." Kane snorted. "Let's just say rodents wouldn't have gone with my mother's décor."

Susannah gave him a curious look and Kane cursed himself for that slip. He should have lied and told her he'd had half a dozen pets. But he was no better at lying than he was at starting a fire, so his best bet was to keep his mouth shut altogether. Except Susannah—when she didn't have that look on her face that said she thought he was either crazy or criminal—had the kind of personality that begged friendliness. Openness.

She had a wide smile, a deep, contagious laugh and luminous green eyes filled with curiosity. They drew him in, making Kane forget his cover story, his life in New York, and had him instead longing for a little of that magic she seemed to possess. The same magic she used to calm dogs, as easily as if she were a human warm blanket and bowl of puppy food.

Perhaps, Kane thought, studying Susannah's bent head, then letting his gaze slip along her lithe form, he could add a little female R & R to his holiday? After all, he was the best man, and she was the maid of honor. They'd have to be together for the wedding. Wasn't it almost expected that they end up sharing a little more than a dance or two?

The golden retriever squirmed under his inattention, sending a river of water down Kane's arm. "You better hold on there," Susannah said with a laugh and a tease in her eyes. "Or I might end up grooming *you* by accident."

"You wouldn't."

She held up the huge water sprayer. "Accidents do happen, you know, all the time in the workplace."

He laughed. "What is this, revenge for this morning?"

"What revenge?" She gave him a look of pure innocence. "I'm just saying—" her finger slipped a teeny bit on the button, sending a quick dribble of water his way "—I'm the one in control of the water here and you better stay on my best side."

The woman didn't seem to have a bad side, at least in the beauty department. From her bright smile to her deep green eyes, to the shapely curves that begged his gaze to slide down her form, everything about Susannah Wilson drew his attention over and over again. Even in jeans and a T-shirt, she looked as beautiful as the runway models he'd known in New York. Maybe even more so, because there was a natural rawness to her looks that set off his libido and had him craving everything about her.

"You're in control, huh?" he said, grinning. Then he stepped to the right, fast, ripping the sprayer from her grip before she even saw him coming. He gave her a quick blast on the belly, and she let out a shriek.

"Hey! No fair."

"All's fair in war and business, didn't you know that?"

Susannah squirmed around in his grip, which brought her directly beneath him, and made Kane very, very aware of their close quarters. Of her parted lips. Of how all it would take would be a breath of a movement, and he could be holding her, having her in his arms, and even more, kissing her.

"Give that back," she said.

"Make me."

She reached for the sprayer. He feinted to the right. She dodged to the left. They collided, closer. Then again, closer still, and both of them froze.

A second ticked by on the clock above. Another. Susannah swallowed. Kane leaned forward, the game forgotten, the sprayer falling into the tub, his hands moving to brace on either side of the stainless steel, when the dog, apparently sensing the distraction of the humans in the room, gave a quick shake, bathing all of them in soapy bubbles.

Kane jerked back. Susannah spun back around and soothed the dog. "We should, ah, get back to work."

"Yeah, we should."

But he knew—and knew she knew—that as much as they might be pretending to return to all business, there'd been a shift between them from just acquaintances to something a little more.

"What made you decide to do this for a living?" he asked,

changing the subject. *Get your mind in the game, Lennox.* Or he'd end up covered in dog and suds, possibly ticking off Susannah—which would mean she'd send him home with that spaniel. Definitely not a win-win. "It's not like dog washing is on the guidance counselor list of career paths."

She bristled slightly. Damn. He'd offended her.

"I'm sorry. I didn't mean—"

"No, it's okay. This is only a temporary gig anyway. I started walking dogs in high school for extra money, and one thing led to another. Before I knew it, I had a business."

"You own The Sudsy Dog?"

She grinned. "All mine, soap bubbles and all."

Yet another surprise. His esteem for her raised several notches. "I'm impressed. Seems like you're doing really well. A one-woman shop and everything. That's not easy to accomplish."

She shrugged. "It's not much."

He reached out, placing a hand on hers, intending only to get her attention, but when his touch slipped against hers because of the soapy water, a zing went up his arm. The charge detonated in his brain, reigniting the sparks from earlier. When was the last time he'd felt that way?

Seven years ago. Rebecca Nichols, a woman Kane had met in his business-ethics class. Rebecca hadn't come from old money or new money, or anything other than a normal apple-pie-eating American family. They'd dated for six months—six fast and furious, amazing months. She'd been the first woman he'd dated who hadn't been handpicked by his father. And Kane had hoped in some crazy way that Elliott would approve. That his father would see his son's choice in a woman as bold. Unique. Carving out his own path. Exactly the qualities Elliott always preached about to his employees—then seemed to do his best to squash in his son.

Kane and Rebecca's relationship had been fun, exciting and perfect—until Elliott Lennox found out his son was dating an "unacceptable" woman and paid Rebecca's family enough money to convince them their daughter would find a better education abroad.

Kane had gotten the message. His father didn't see his son as bold or determined. Simply headstrong and foolish, particularly when it came to women. Stepping out of line with the family plan would cost him. Dearly. The business and the family image came above everything, even personal happiness.

Kane had been allowed to stay at Northwestern, but only after agreeing to tightly toe the Lennox family line. And the price Kane had to pay? His father sent him a new roommate—to make sure Kane stayed in line.

Now, here he was, for the first time in forever, feeling a powerful surge of attraction again. Real, honest desire. For a real, honest woman, not the kind who put on social airs. Damn, it felt good. Real good. Kane caught Susannah's gaze. Had she been affected, like he?

But no. She gave him a look as blank as a clean slate, waiting for him to speak. Kane tried to refocus, to remind himself he was here for a short vacation, a work reprieve, not a major life departure. He cleared his throat. "It's a lot, believe me. Up to fifty percent of all new businesses fail within the first five years. You should be proud."

Now her gaze narrowed. "How do you know so much about business?"

Damn. He had yet to learn the keys to a good cover story. Keep your mouth shut and know your lines.

He couldn't very well rattle off his real résumé. Kane

Lennox: fourth-generation CEO of the largest gem importing company in the world. Kane Lennox, one of *the* Lennoxes, the family that had been listed in the *Forbes 500* issue for as many years as the magazine had been printed. Kane Lennox: the man with enough personal fortune to buy this town ten times over and still have change left over to line the streets with thousand-dollar bills.

If he told her any of that, she'd look at him just like everyone else did. With awe. With reverence. She'd step back and stop seeing him as just Kane. And for the first time in his life, he wanted to just be—

Kane.

Ordinary man. In ordinary clothes. Doing ordinary things. With no butlers. No limos. No expectations.

"I, ah, just like to read business magazines," he said finally. "When I'm not at work. You know, in the spirit of getting ahead."

"That I can understand." A soft smile of empathy stole across her face. "Working hard for what you want, right?"

"Exactly."

"That's my personal philosophy, too." She shot him a grin. "Who'd have thought I would have anything in common with a guy I met on my sister's lawn?"

He echoed her grin. "A barefoot guy at that."

She laughed. "And here I usually go for the kind who wear shoes."

"I'll keep that in—" The dog wriggled then, shaking off the soapy water, spraying the room, Susannah and Kane with a fine sheen of bubbles. Kane backed up, warding off the foamy onslaught, cursing under his breath. But that only seemed to encourage the golden dog, who shook even more vigorously, her tail becoming a soap-spraying fan.

"What is *wrong* with that animal?"

Susannah laughed. "If you held on to her, she won't do that."

"What do you think I was doing? She's not cooperating."

Susannah arched a brow.

"Hey, if you think you can do a better job holding—" Kane said, backing up and waving at the dog.

"Fine. I'll do your job and you can do mine."

"What are you talking about?"

"You can wash." She tossed a bottle of shampoo at him and moved away from the dog's head.

"No. No, I didn't mean I'd…" Kane stared at the bottle, then the animal, then Susannah, then the dog again. "There is absolutely no way I can wash this animal."

"A deal's a deal, isn't it? You said you'd help. You haven't been much help so far." She gave him a grin that was more of a challenge. And again, his libido roared to life. "Besides, Dakota here isn't so bad. Trust me. She's one of the easier clients I have."

"Easier?" Kane snorted disagreement. He looked at the dog again. The dog looked at him, her wide soulful brown eyes seeming to say, "Oh, no, not him." Kane took in a deep breath, squirted a little shampoo into his hands, then rubbed them together. "Uh, where do I…?"

"Her back. Just scrub it in, using your nails to really get in good under the coat. Think of it like a doggie massage."

Kane made a face. He'd rather massage a person than a dog any day. Specifically the female person beside him. He imagined his touch running down her body, over those luscious curves, followed by his lips, lingering along her long neck—

Definitely not thoughts he should be having when he should be helping her at work. He couldn't help it. Susannah

Wilson had intrigued him—even if she had put him to work on the least fun end of the dog. "Doggie massage?"

"Hey, dogs like TLC, too."

Kane didn't want to do anything resembling a doggie massage, but he also didn't want that stray hanging around his cabin, so he'd suck it up and do what Susannah asked. He leaned forward, splayed his fingers and sunk them into the dog's deep fur. The dog wriggled against his touch, and seemed to almost…smile.

Beneath his fingers, the retriever's fur was thick and heavy, but it parted easily, allowing him access to the animal's skin. He gave Susannah a dubious glance; she offered him an encouraging smile, and he dug in, doing his best to offer—

A soapy doggie massage, as insane as that sounded.

Yet his thoughts kept returning to the blond human beside him. Susannah started humming snippets of an old sixties tune, her hips swaying with the rhythm, her hair catching the dance, as if her whole body was part of the concert. So natural, so uninhibited. So different from anyone he'd ever met.

"I hear people find TLC rewarding, as well," Kane said.

"Mmm-hmm." Susannah stopped humming and stroked the dog behind the ears instead. "That's a good girl, Dakota. Just a few more minutes, pup."

But Kane wasn't thinking about the canine at all. His thoughts were entirely focused on Susannah. In a few days, the two of them would be at a wedding together, which meant he'd be escorting her down the aisle, then dancing with her at the reception. Holding her in his arms. The anticipation drummed in his veins.

Maybe…he didn't need to wait that long. He could ask her out and—

His cell phone began to chirp, its annoying ring cutting through the room like a bullhorn.

"Do you want me to get that for you?" Susannah asked.

"Ignore it. I'm on vacation. Apparently not everyone got the memo." His assistant was supposed to redirect all calls, but a few must have gotten past her eagle eyes. Either that, or his father was already noting his absence. Regardless, Kane refused to be reattached to the business umbilical already.

He had more important things to attend to right this second. Things like Susannah Wilson.

"Speaking of people TLC...do you know a place in this town that has good food? For people, not dogs." He gave her a grin. "I think I have the dog menu all covered."

"You can get great takeout at the Corner Kitchen over on Main and Newberry. The owner makes homemade everything, from strawberry jam to mashed potatoes. It's nothing gourmet, but—"

Kane chuckled. "To me, that'll be exotic, trust me."

She gave him a curious look. "How can mashed potatoes and strawberry jam be exotic?"

He directed his attention to the dog again, using the overhead sprayer to rinse out the shampoo, and to avoid looking at Susannah. Damn. Good thing he'd never gone into the CIA. His cover could have been blown by a three-year-old. "I, ah, eat out a lot. You know, all that nonhomemade food. The Corner Kitchen will be a real treat. I haven't had food like that since I was a little kid." Actually, he'd never had any of that kind of food, but at least saying "since I was a little kid" sounded plausible.

"Did you have an aunt or something who liked to cook?"

"Something like that." A maid. Who'd fixed gourmet meals at his parents' beck and call. And after that, a host of restaurants that served five-star meals, none of which had strawberry jam or sweet-potato pies on the menu.

"What about you? Do you have dinner plans?"

"I'm busy tonight, sorry."

The brush-off came as fast as a bucket of ice water. Something new for him—a woman turning him down so quickly. That must come with the incognito territory.

And instead of depressing Kane, the words invigorated him. Issued a challenge, of sorts. He had finally met a woman who didn't know who he was, had no interest in his money—because she didn't even know it existed. How many women had he met, who had looked at him with dollar signs in their eyes? They saw his money first, and him last, if at all.

All his life he'd wanted to meet a woman—meet people in general—who connected with him for *him*, not for his fortune. Not for his name. He'd thought he'd done that back in college, until his father had yanked the relationship away, with that all-powerful dollar. All Kane had ever wanted from his father was a relationship, but he'd only received criticism and money. Even now, his father was back in New York, probably in the Lennox Gem Corporation boardroom, raising a holy fit over the fact that he had no idea where his son was right now. Not because he cared, but because he'd lost control of the reins.

Which left Kane free to pursue Susannah Wilson, if he wanted to. If she did date him, even only for the few days he'd be here, it wouldn't be because he was Kane Lennox. Or because she hoped to be draped in diamonds by the end of the week. Not because of anything other than she truly liked him.

A curl of desire ran through Kane, a feeling so new, it was

almost foreign. It awakened a hunger he hadn't felt in so long, he thought he might have imagined it all those years ago.

Beside his feet, the stray dog, which Susannah had started calling Rover, raised his snout and let out a little bark. "I think someone else wants a bath, now that Dakota's about done," Susannah said. "We could always do a two-for-one today."

"Sorry. One dog's my limit."

"You did a good job," Susannah said a minute later, thankfully taking Kane's place and allowing him back into doing leash-holding duty. "Dakota's nice and clean. Maybe I'll offer you a job."

"I have one, thank you."

"What do you do?"

"I'm, ah, in the jewelry business." He left it at that. No telling her he imported billions of dollars worth of diamonds and precious gems.

"Really? Do you work in a shop, too?"

"Uh, sort of."

The last of the suds ran down the drain, and Dakota, sensing the end of her bath, began to shake. Susannah tightened her grasp on the leash, and calmed the dog with a few soothing words.

"If you want, I can bring Rover closer, and then we can get that two-for-one," Kane said.

She laughed. For the first time, he noticed how easily her laughter came, how light the sound was, almost like chimes. The animation in her face brought a lightness to him, too, like spreading sunshine. "Now, there's a great business idea. Almost like assembly-line dog washing." She reached over the tub for a giant hose and turned it on, blowing a steady stream of warm air on the dog. In minutes, the retriever was nearly dry.

A teenage girl breezed into the shop, dumping an over-stuffed neon-pink backpack into a chair as she did. Her brown hair, tied back in a ponytail with a blue-and-gold ribbon, swung back and forth as she bounced over to the cage holding the standard poodle. "Sorry I'm late, Suzie," she called over her shoulder. "Hey, Dakota. Hi, Fancy Pants." She cooed at the white dog, unlatching the cage and opening the door enough to give the dog a little head scratch.

Then, as if Kane was a lesser species that she had just noticed, the teenager latched the poodle's cage and sent Kane a half nod. "Oh, hi. Who are you?"

"This is Kane. Kane, meet Tess."

He greeted the girl, but she had already bent down and started petting Rover. "Do you belong to him? He's a cutie."

"No, no. *No.*"

Tess grinned when Rover perked up at the sound of Kane's voice and darted over to his side. "Seems he disagrees."

Susannah opened the gate on the side of the tub, helped Dakota down, then led the retriever over to a grooming table in the next room. Kane took Rover out to the front of the shop. With the distance of a room between them, relief whispered through Susannah. Working so close to Kane had set her on edge.

She'd been aware of his every move, of the water droplets on his skin, of the way his muscles flexed when he'd worked the soap into Dakota's coat. She needed distance from him, from the senses he'd awakened. Most of all, she needed to redouble her focus on her job—and her ultimate goals.

"Tess, do you mind finishing up Dakota and then holding down the fort alone for a little while? There's only one more appointment left for the day."

"Not at all." Tess slipped a Sudsy Dog apron over her

head and helped Susannah get Dakota into place on the grooming table, then readied nail clippers and brushes. "Let me guess. You have ten thousand errands to do for other people."

Susannah smiled, but the grin seemed to droop. "Only nine thousand and ninety nine."

"Just say no. That's what they teach us in health class." She grinned.

"That might work with randy teenage boys, but not when it comes to my sister. She's—"

"Needy. And you're too nice to turn anyone down." Tess patted her on the arm. "I know, I know, I should keep my mouth shut and respect my elders and all that."

"No, you're right." Susannah sighed. One of these days, maybe Jackie would get it and stop relying so much on Susannah. She knew she should simply stop *doing* for her sister, but that was easier said than done. She'd gotten so used to watching out for Jackie, to being both mother and father, that turning that instinct off was nearly impossible. Susannah took her apron off and hung it on a hook. "Anyway, I better get going. I'll be back to walk the shelter dogs later tonight."

"No problem. Me and Fancy Pants and Dakota will put on some Rolling Stones and have a great time. A real party." Tess winked.

Susannah was still laughing when she reached the main part of the shop, where Kane and Rover waited. "Thanks again, Kane. I appreciate your help today."

"Not a favor. A deal, remember?" He handed her the leash, collar and dog food she had given him earlier. "Thank *you* for taking my problem off my hands."

"It wasn't a problem." She smiled. "At all."

When Susannah's gaze met Kane's, a part of him wondered if she was talking about the dog. Or dealing with him. Or something else.

Dating Susannah Wilson could certainly be a great part of his vacation. She was a fiery, beautiful woman, one who had captivated his attention. By spending time with her, perhaps his days in Chapel Ridge would be a lot more entertaining than he'd expected—and come with a few extra perks, beyond a couple of days alone in the woods, time that allowed him to temporarily leave the problems of his real life far behind.

But as Kane left and the door to Susannah's shop shut behind him, he felt something brush up against his leg. Kane looked down and saw the little barrel of brown-and-white fur, right beside him, a determined stowaway. Apparently, leaving his problems behind wasn't going to be as easy as he'd thought.

CHAPTER FOUR

"You are a saint."

Susannah laughed. "Far from it. I'm just helping Jackie."

Kim Sheldon put a fist on her hip and arched a brow. Curvy and brunette, Kim brought her straight, no-nonsense approach to everything from her conversations to her jeans and in-your-face T-shirt logos. Today's read Get Your Ducks In A Row…And Keep Them Outta My Pond.

"Story of your life, Suzie." Kim reached into one of the boxes and pulled out a squat glass bowl, then placed it on the round table. "Tell me again why you're here instead of at the bachelorette party. I mean, that *is* one of the duties of the maid of honor, too, you know. To get rip-roarin' drunk and embarrass herself with a really hunky male stripper."

"I don't have a whole lot in common with those girls."

"What's to have in common? You look at the sexy guys, toss out some dollar bills and throw back some Long Island iced teas." Kim grinned. "For some people, that's the basis of a lifelong friendship."

"Jackie didn't need me there. She needed me here." Susannah opened a bag of clear glass beads, poured several dozen into the bowl, then began arranging light blue and white artificial flowers in the center. After the flowers were set, she draped silver ribbons along the edges of bowl, giving the centerpiece a touch of shimmer.

Kim put a hand on Susannah's as she reached for another bowl with her opposite hand. "She asked you to *pick* the centerpieces up, not *set* them up. So what gives with the big avoidance deal?"

Susannah sighed and sank into one of the cranberry flocked chairs. "Jackie's friends have really never been mine. Every time I'm around them, I feel like a fifth wheel. A square one at that."

"But why? You're just as accomplished as any of them."

"Kim, I *wash dogs* for a living. That's not exactly achieving my full potential."

Kim gave her friend a one-armed hug. "To the dogs, it is. They love you, and so do your customers. Heck, you started when you were eleven, and now look at you. You have your own shop, no debt, an appointment book so full it threatens to explode on a daily basis—"

"While my sister's friends are all married to doctors and lawyers and driving around town in SUVs, talking about their designer baby bags. I'm not just a bridesmaid, Kim, I'm the proverbial old maid of the group." Every time she tried to talk to her sister's friends, the conversations died midstream. Susannah felt like she had yet to experience life, had yet to reach beyond the borders of this small town.

"Jackie's friends are not that bad."

Susannah paused in filling another bowl and traced a circle into the white tablecloth. "No, they're not. I'm just grumpy, I guess. Anxious to get out of town."

"To live your life. Not everyone else's."

"Exactly." She looked up into Kim's understanding brown eyes. "I've waited so long for this chance. Now that Jackie is getting married…"

"You feel like it's your turn."

Susannah nodded.

Kim's hand covered hers again. "Maybe it was your turn a long time ago. Did you ever consider that?"

"What do you mean?"

"Jackie's twenty-two. An adult, Suzie. You stopped being responsible for her a long time ago."

Except that mantle had never left Susannah's shoulders. She'd worn the heaviness like a thick winter coat every day of her life since their parents had died eight years ago and at only eighteen herself, she'd been left in charge of fourteen-year-old Jackie. Jackie had grown up, but that hadn't stopped Susannah from worrying, from feeling as if she should stay around one more day, one more hour, and keep on watching out for her not-always-responsible younger sister. "You're right, but…"

"But you don't always take your own advice." Kim smiled. "When the wedding's over, promise me you'll stop being such a mother hen."

"Definitely. I'm going on a long, long, long trip. Three weeks in Paris by myself. You never know," she added, grinning, "I might love it so much, I might not come back."

"Leave this town forever? You?" Kim scoffed. "I don't think so. You love it here. Everyone who lives here loves you, too."

Susannah rose and stretched out her arms, spinning as she did, as if she could shake all that off. "I want to see the world, Kim. I want to see what else is out there. I want…" She heaved a sigh. "I want to experience everything."

Kim laughed. "What you want is to hit the lottery to pay for these big dreams."

Susannah lowered her arms and nodded. "Yeah, I do. But at least I can take a trip, then come back here and say

I did that, saw that, experienced this. It's a start. And it can tide me over for a long time while I'm living in an apartment and saving for the next trip. It will get me through the next four hundred poodles." She grinned, then went back to the boxes.

Kim's cell phone rang. She checked the number. "Damn. Speaking of family, that's my mom. I'm late picking her up. She has a doctor's appointment and I promised to run her over there." Kim's gaze swept the stacks of boxes, the piles of tablecloths waiting to be laid out—another money-saving step Jackie had volunteered to take on but left in Susannah's lap. "I hate to leave you with all this."

"Go, go. I'll be fine. Seriously."

"That's what you always say, you glutton for punishment." Kim gave her friend a quick hug. "Promise me you won't stay too late. I'll call you when I'm done, and if you're still here, I'll zip back and finish up with you, 'kay?"

"Sure."

Kim hurried out of the ballroom. Quiet descended over the vast room, broken only by the occasional sound of the hotel's staff working in the kitchen beyond the doors. The Chapel Ridge Hotel was small—and not much of a hotel, considering its location in the itty-bitty town. But it had a view of the lake, and because of that, the hotel did a brisk wedding and prom business.

To keep their costs low, Jackie and Paul had chosen to hold their wedding on a Friday in mid-April, before the busy season began. The owner, the father of one of Jackie's high-school classmates, had given the young couple a break on the price and as many bonuses—like a few extra days for setup—that he could.

Susannah dropped into one of the chairs, her leg muscles aching from the long day spent standing, and got busy assembling the centerpieces. The work became mindless. Dumping in the glass marbles, assembling the silk flowers, adding the ribbons. She worked in assembly-line fashion, creating four at a time—all that she had room for on the space before her.

Halfway through the chore, she started counting, then realized she had left another box in the trunk. Damn. All she really wanted to do after a long day at The Sudsy Dog was sit down and stay sitting down. Instead, she pushed off from the table and headed outside.

Once at her car, Susannah wrangled her arms around the heavy box, but the cardboard had wedged itself into the trunk and refused to budge. She turned her face up to the April sun, catching the weak rays, and wished she could insta-port herself to a beach.

"You look like you could use a hand."

Susannah started. Kane stood behind her, leaning against his rental car. He'd traded his T-shirt for a button-down shirt, this one as neatly pressed as a shirt fresh from the dry cleaners. The light blue of the oxford set off the cobalt of his eyes, and for a second, Susannah forgot to breathe. The sun bathed him in a bright golden light, casting glints across the slight waves of his short dark hair. If she didn't find him so aggravating, she'd be forced to admit he was incredibly attractive.

Okay, he *was* incredibly attractive.

"I've got it under—" She cut herself off. Hadn't she had enough of shouldering all the burden? Of doing all the work and constantly saying she was fine? Hadn't Kim told her basically the same thing just a few minutes ago? If she didn't start standing up for herself now, when was she going to? "Yes, I do need some help. Thanks."

He pushed off from the car, his strides confident, purposeful, a man who clearly commanded every situation he entered. He crossed to her, then reached inside the trunk and worked the box back and forth until it was free. From her position behind him, Susannah couldn't help but notice how well his jeans fit, hugging his body as if they'd been custom made. That sizzle of attraction ran through her again, this time at a hotter and faster pace.

"Damn," he said. "What's in here?"

"The last of twenty-five glass centerpieces. And the marbles and things that go in them."

"Feels more like twenty-five elephants." Nevertheless, Kane hefted the container easily in his grip, as if it weighed no more than a box of feathers. "Where's it going?"

"I can—" Suzie cut off the sentence, then pointed toward the building before them. He was offering to carry, and her tired arms and legs were more than willing to take him up on that offer. "Inside the ballroom here. The hotel is letting me set up early. The owners are friends of my parents and they don't have any other events in that room before the wedding."

"Why are you doing this? Isn't it normally the wedding coordinator's job?" He fell into step beside her.

Susannah scoffed. "Wedding coordinator? That's a little out of Jackie and Paul's budget. As it is, they're pinching every penny they can."

"But why you? What about Paul? Or Jackie? The bridesmaids? Or the mother of the bride?"

The arrow pierced Susannah's heart with no warning, taking her breath with a searing pain. Her parents had been gone for eight years, and in all that time, she'd worked so hard to keep her emotions in check, to keep that part of herself under control.

But that one little phrase, "mother of the bride," had slammed into her with a reminder of how much she and

Jackie had lost—and how much more Frank and Eleanor Wilson had never seen happen—and never would.

Susannah swallowed hard, locking those thoughts deep in her mental closet, then pulled open the Chapel Ridge Hotel door and held it as Kane entered the building. "The, uh, ballroom is down the hall and to the right."

"And the topic is closed."

"Yep." Susannah slipped in front of him and led the way to the ballroom, then opened one of the double doors. "You can put it on the banquet table. I've got it from here. I'm almost done, anyway."

He deposited the box beside several others marked Wedding Decorations. Then he stepped back and assessed the mass of unassembled bowls, the bags of beads, the jumbled piles of waiting silk flowers. "Are you planning on doing all this yourself?"

"That wasn't the plan, but yeah, that's how it worked out. Tonight's the bachelorette party, so the other bridesmaids are all taking Jackie out."

"While the maid of honor stays behind and plays Cinderella?"

Cinderella. Maybe that moniker had described her life until now, but Susannah intended to have her time at the ball. Soon. Just not today. Susannah avoided his gaze and started unpacking the box. "It's not like that. I'm not much of a partier, that's all."

He arched a brow and didn't say anything.

Susannah unfolded a tablecloth and spread it across a round table, smoothing the white surface with her palm. "I thought you were headed for the woods. For your cabin by the lake. You and your new best friend."

"I had a couple other errands to run first. Then I saw you and…here I am."

What other errand? she wanted to ask, but didn't. Again, she reminded herself she wasn't here to get to know him better, even as every instinct in her body told her this man was hiding some serious secrets. Everything about Kane Lennox spelled brooding, dark, mysterious. How on earth could gregarious, blue-collar Paul have ever hooked up with someone like Kane, a man who seemed so far removed from Paul's element, he might as well have been on another planet? "So where's your dog?"

"He's not my dog. And he's sleeping in the car." Kane met her inquisitive gaze. "Yes, I did leave a window cracked. All four of them, for that matter. I'm not completely clueless."

"I never said you were. In fact, you seem like an awfully smart guy." She reached into the box for a second tablecloth, but before she could unfurl it, Kane was there, holding the opposite end. He helped her lay the cloth on the table and palm it into shape. "You met Paul in college?"

"Yes."

"Did you get a degree in history, too?"

Kane chuckled. "No. History was my downfall. The only reason I passed it at all was Paul. In fact, that's where I met him—in Warfare Theory and Strategy."

Susannah returned to her worktable and took a seat before the mass of centerpieces yet to be constructed. "If you weren't good at history, why take a class like that? It sounds a lot more complex than World History 101."

"It was. I took it because it was my duty." At her gesture, Kane handed her a package of trim, lowering himself into the seat beside Susannah.

"For what? The army?"

He chuckled. "Sort of. My family duty. I wanted a certain type of degree, and knew which classes would best fit that, hence the Warfare Theory and Strategy class. My father is a rather exacting man, and he didn't agree *at all* with my choice of college, so I made sure all my class choices lived up to his standards."

Susannah's fingers stilled, silver ribbon suspended midway to the next bowl. "Wow. He was that hard on you? But you…you were what, eighteen already?"

"In my family," Kane said quietly, "age is never a consideration when it comes to duty. And failure is never an option. So I was very grateful for Paul's help in history."

"Never fail?" she echoed softly. She'd grown up in a family that had encouraged every achievement, no matter how small; belittled nothing. She couldn't imagine having that kind of pressure on her shoulders as a child.

Kane went on as if he hadn't heard her. "Paul sat next to me, and not only was he the class clown, something I really needed at that time in my life, but he seemed to know his history better than anyone. He saved my butt more than once."

"Paul *is* a bit of a comedian. It's what makes him such a popular teacher at the high school."

"That I can see." Kane smiled, then handed her a package of beads.

Susannah opened the bag and began pouring the clear beads into a vase. "So was your major also family dictated?"

He cocked an elbow on the table and studied her. "You really like playing twenty questions, don't you?"

"Don't you think we should get to know each other better? I mean, we are going to be latched together for the wedding."

That was her excuse and she was sticking to it. Her interest had nothing to do with the simmering attraction between them. Nothing to do with the way he studied her, or how watching him touch the silk petals had made her swallow, thinking of those same fingers against her own skin. Nothing to do with the way Kane Lennox had awakened something in her that she hadn't expected.

He laid the silk flowers in his hand down on the table. "Is that all? Just trying to get to know the guy you're going to be stuck with for a few hours at a reception?"

Nothing to do with the way looking at him made her wonder if she'd been missing out on something all these years. If Miss Responsibility should take a little vacation—before her vacation.

Susannah inhaled, and when she did, she caught the citrus notes of his cologne. The quiet undertone of man, the low, unmistakable hum of sexual current. "Of course."

Liar.

His hand inched closer to hers on the table, separated now by only the thin paper-wrapped wire stem of the faux rose. The paper rustled against her skin, nerve endings springing awake like crocuses suddenly blossoming under a new sun. "For this week, I'm here on vacation," Kane said, his voice low and quiet, as if whispering a secret meant only for her ears, "and that means I don't want to talk about my job or where I'm from or anything from my ordinary life. I just want to be Kane."

"Okay…Kane."

"And while I'm sure it would be wonderful…" at that, his voice dipped into an even lower range "…to know every last detail about you, I think it would be even more fun to maintain the mystery. So how about I remain just Kane, and you are simply—" his smile quirked up "—Susannah."

Not Susannah the sister, expected to tidy up all the messes. Not Susannah the business owner, working dozens of hours to save for a dream that seemed so far away. Not

Susannah the town daughter, who had always been so responsible, so perfect. Just Susannah—

A stranger. No expectations on her shoulders. No one waiting for her to do anything except, as Kane had said, have fun.

Fun. The one thing she'd been waiting to have nearly all her life.

The idea thrilled her. Excited her. Opened up a possibility Susannah had thought was closed to a small-town girl with a sister to raise, at least until she journeyed to the other side of the world. But maybe, for a few days at least, she could be just Susannah, and see what that would be like.

She put out her hand. "Pleased to meet you, Kane."

Kane's larger hand engulfed hers, his warm palm sending a burst of heat through her body. The insane desire to kiss him surged in Susannah's gut.

She jerked back, away from him. Whoa. This was going way beyond a simple game of pretending to be someone other than herself. Regardless, she did have responsibilities, did have people waiting on her. And did have seven gazillion beads to pour into bowls.

"I, ah, need to get back to work."

A smile crossed his face. "I recognize that trait."

"What trait?" Susannah turned to the table, opening another package of beads and pouring them into the next bowl.

Kane waited until the last bead had finished its tinkling journey into the bowl with its fellow clear friends before speaking. "Workaholic. Type A. Never on vacation. Never taking a break."

"You must have me confused with someone else, because I am definitely not—" She stopped jabbing the flowers into the beads. "Well, maybe a little. But I have a reason for all this."

In a mirror to her actions, Kane opened up some beads and filled a bowl, then began repeating her, flower for flower. "Let me guess. World domination of the dog-grooming industry? Or you're saving to launch a wedding-planner business?"

"None of the above." She slid a pile of the silver bead strings over to Kane, then demonstrated how to attach them, finishing off the centerpiece. "I'm just…saving for the future."

"I recognize that trait. The 'I'm keeping my personal cards close to my chest.' I'm like that, too."

She laughed. "I don't think we're anything like each other. At all."

"You don't." The words came out as a statement, not a question.

"For one, I don't go around barefoot on people's lawns."

"You've never gone barefoot in the grass?"

"Well, of course I've done that. But—"

"Well, I haven't." He pushed the finished centerpiece away, drew a new bowl toward him and set to work again. His work was as efficient and neat as his attire. No wasted movements or time.

"You haven't…what? Walked barefoot on grass?" Her jaw dropped. "But everyone's done that."

"Not everyone has lived the same life you do, Susannah." The beads made their plink-plink journey down, forcing a pause in the conversation.

"Did you grow up in a city or something? Live in an apartment without a yard?"

A muscle twitched in his jaw. "Something like that."

"And is that why you came here? To the middle of the country? To basically Nowhereville?"

"I came here because…" Kane paused, and drew in a breath "…this town is as far removed from my life as you can get. It's…perfect."

"That's all?" Susannah heard a hole in the sentence, though, something left out, like a puzzle piece forgotten under a sofa cushion. Or a closet door locked to keep out prying guests.

"That's all." A smile crossed his face. "And that's all I want to say today, Just Susannah."

She smiled back. "Okay, Just Kane."

But as they got back to work, Kane's words tumbled in Susannah's mind. He'd said they shared similar traits, as if he had her all figured out. But he didn't. Susannah had little in common with this neatly pressed man who clearly came from the other side of the tracks. He lived in a world so unlike her own he couldn't possibly understand her, or have anything in common with her. Or understand her driving need to work—so she could leave the very town he'd purposely sought for his vacation.

They worked for another half hour, exchanging little more than small talk about Chapel Ridge, its residents, and the fishing at Lake Everett this time of year. The bowls got filled, the flowers were placed, the tables were set, and before Susannah knew it, the room was ready. In a quarter of the time she'd expected the chore to take. Kane's cell phone rang incessantly, even though he'd turned it to vibrate. He didn't answer a single call, merely looked at the caller ID display, and then went on with his conversation with Susannah, as if the phone had never interrupted.

She rubbed at a kink in her neck. At the same time, her stomach let out a low rumble, a reminder that she had skipped dinner. Again. "Thanks for your help. I really appreciate it. You saved me hours of time."

"Did you eat yet?" Kane asked.

Her face flushed. He had heard that. "I will."

"Let me guess. Takeout, alone, at your kitchen table, or in front of the television."

"Well…" Susannah thought of lying, then found it impossible to do so when her gaze met Kane's piercing blue eyes. He had a way of looking at a woman that seemed to capture her every thought. "That's the usual approach, yes."

"Mine, too. How about we both break with tradition and—" he paused, then a slight grin came over his face "—eat together?"

"Together?" she echoed.

"No strings, no date. No 'expectations.'" He framed the words with air quotes. "Just two people sharing a table."

Her stomach rumbled again, offering an answer before Susannah could voice an objection. Exhaustion sat heavy on her shoulders, the long day, added on top of dozens and dozens of long days, catching up with her like weight on a rope. The thought of sitting alone at home—again—didn't sound as appealing as it normally did. In fact, it sounded depressing. When was the last time she'd been out on a date?

Way too long ago, that was for sure.

Besides, hadn't she vowed she was going to change her life, starting in a few days? What better way to do that than to change her habits? Step out of her rut?

Except…every time she looked at Kane, a mental alarm bell began to ring. Kane Lennox may have piqued her interest with this "Just Kane" and "Just Susannah" game, but Susannah Wilson lived in the real world, one that wasn't going to go away, not until she hopped on that plane.

Any thoughts of tangling with the fire this stranger represented should be put on hold. Set aside, for later. Or better yet, never.

Because there was something there, something that kept nagging at the back of her mind. Kane Lennox may be Paul's friend, and he may have been working really hard at coming across as just another vacationer, but something told Susannah there was more going on.

But what? It wasn't like people came to Chapel Ridge looking for hot investment properties. Or to seek out long-lost family members. The small town held no dark secrets, hidden treasures or incognito celebrities. She shook off her suspicions. Kane Lennox was here for the wedding and a few days off, nothing more. In that time frame, surely, he didn't expect to kindle anything with her or anyone else who lived in this town.

Even if a part of her wanted to kindle something—the very crazy part, the part that clearly kept forgetting a relationship was *not* on her agenda. Regardless of Kane's hotness level.

It wasn't a date, as he'd said. So she shouldn't worry one way or another about anything. About fire, or kindling or the way something stirred inside her every time Kane Lennox looked at her with that intense stare of his.

She glanced down at her jeans and T-shirt. "I'm not really dressed for dinner."

"That's okay. I was thinking something more…casual." He grinned.

"Casual?" She arched a brow. "As in what?"

"As in trust a stranger."

That was the only problem—she didn't trust him. Not even a little. And what was more—she wasn't trusting herself, or her reactions to him, a whole lot right now, either.

CHAPTER FIVE

"IF THIS is what you call 'just dinner,' I can only imagine how fancy a real date would be."

Kane heard the tease in Susannah's voice, saw it in the way she wagged the hot dog at him, and he felt himself smile and relax for the first time in…well, forever. There was something about this woman that seemed to set him at ease, even as being with her forced him to remain on guard, to remember his place—and who he was, or rather wasn't, supposed to be.

He kept forgetting all of the above, every time he talked to her. Telling her how he'd grown up without ever stepping barefoot on the grass, how he'd never had a pet…he might as well just go around with a Hello, My Name is Kane Lennox and I'm a Billionaire badge.

But so far she didn't seem to recognize him. Most people didn't—unless they read the gem trade magazines, *Forbes* or the *Wall Street Journal.* Or if he put on a suit and got behind the wheel of his Bentley. Then he might as well advertise his heritage.

He had to rehearse his cover story better. Bored corporate exec, here for a little fresh air, some fishing. Saw an opportunity for both when Paul's wedding came up. Nothing more.

Now he and Susannah sat beneath the shadow of a red-and-white-striped umbrella, at a hard plastic picnic table, eating from paper rectangular containers filled with something called Coney dogs and French fries. A sense of liberation ran through Kane, even as he blocked his arteries with another bite, and upped his cholesterol with a second order of fries. "This is not my usual dinner," he said. And thank God for that. If he had to sit through one more dinner party of duck confit and asparagus with Hollandaise sauce, he'd scream.

"Let me guess," Susannah said, leaning back to feed an eager, tail-wagging Rover a tidbit of a hamburger patty Kane had ordered just for the dog, "you're usually eating a bowl of cereal while you watch the news. Or is it delivered pizza with a football game on the big screen?"

He bit back a laugh. He couldn't even conjure up the mental image of himself sitting on the thirty-thousand-dollar leather sofa in his vast great room, eating a greasy pizza. All his life, his homes had held a person who cooked Kane's meals, served the dinners to him on priceless china, then whisked the dishes away with silent precision, keeping his home as pristine as his business's ledgers. Before today, he'd never ordered something as mundane as a hot dog and fries, never imagined himself eating al fresco in a loud and tacky outdoor diner.

But if he told Susannah any of that, he'd raise her suspicions for sure. "Greasy pizza and football, that's me."

He was half tempted to add a few grunts, just for good measure. Manly man. Oof-oof.

She cocked her head and studied him, her deep green eyes drawing him, enticing Kane to open his world to her. "Greasy pizza, huh? Is that why you have your napkin in your lap? Why you used a fork to eat your fries?"

He looked down and realized he had, indeed, done that very thing, while all around him, people were eating the meal with their fingers. Damn. He couldn't have stuck out more if he'd draped himself in a red cape. "My, ah, mother was a big stickler for manners."

Understatement of the year, considering his mother had brought in every available descendant of Emily Post to teach young Kane decorum lessons.

Susannah laughed, and the light, airy sound again reminded him of chimes. "I guess so. Boy, did you miss out on a lot, then. Half the fun of fries is getting ketchup and salt on your fingers."

Half the fun. As he looked at her, at her smile, the light in her eyes, Kane could feel the fun emanating from Susannah Wilson like the heat from her body. She was right. He'd been missing exactly that—and had come here hoping to find that kind of fun. Thus far, all he'd found was a dog he didn't want. If he ever expected this to work, he needed to do what Susannah had said—and get a little ketchup on his fingers.

So, even though it rebelled against every ounce of decorum bred into his society blue blood, Kane put down the fork, picked up the red plastic ketchup bottle and gave it a squeeze. Nothing came out. He squeezed harder, and still the nozzle remained dry.

"Give it a shake," Susannah suggested. "Then try again."

He did as she said. Almost.

Ketchup sprayed across the fries, the tabletop, his Coney dog, and Kane's shirt, dotting everything like a crime scene. Even Rover got a glop. The dog let out a yelp, jumped back, then turned and started licking at his fur with his built-in tongue washing machine.

Kane cursed, reaching for the pile of napkins, trying to

control the tomato carnage. But Susannah started laughing. "You squeezed and shook at the same time, silly. And you did it like a man."

"Like a man?"

"Yeah, with the strength of the Incredible Hulk. It's a ketchup bottle, not a he-man contest. Here, let me help you." She reached out, took some of the napkins, and in an instant, had the table mess cleaned up.

He glanced down. "The table's good, but I look like the victim of a serial killer."

Susannah leaned forward, dipping her napkin first in a bit of water and began to dab at his shirt. Her long hair draped across her face, shielding part of her cheek, her eye, from his view. He reached up and pushed the locks back, and she paused, her gaze connecting with his. Kane's heart began to pound harder. He would have kissed her, but they were in a public place, and he swore half the town was watching them.

"I, ah, don't think that's going to do it," he said, gesturing to his shirt. "Is there a dry cleaner nearby?"

Susannah pulled back, moving to tuck her hair back, just as Kane had wanted to. A slight flush filled her cheeks. "There is, but Abe closes up shop before noon on Thursdays. It's his fishing day."

"You're kidding me. Who runs a business that way?"

"Someone who doesn't believe in working himself to death. Abe's almost seventy, and the dry-cleaning thing is only a part-time job."

"Then why doesn't he hire in some help? Then he could stay open later."

She smiled and waved at the full tables. "Look around you. This town isn't exactly overrun with people who need dry cleaning."

True, Chapel Ridge had that exact kick-back-and-put-your-feet-up air about it that had made him choose to stay here. Few people he'd seen out and about had been dressed in anything fancier than jeans and a T-shirt.

"I'm sorry I couldn't get out the stain," Susannah said, reaching out again with the napkin, then pulling back at the last second as if she'd thought better of the gesture. "I'm afraid all my dabbing only made it worse."

She hadn't made anything worse except his attraction to her.

"It's okay. I'll just buy a new shirt."

"Or you can wash that out. It'll just take a little elbow grease."

"Wash it out?" he repeated.

"Sure. Just put on some pretreatment and throw it in the washer—" She put a hand on her forehead. "That's right. You're staying in the cabins at the lake. You don't have a washer there, which means you'd have to go to the laundromat. And for one shirt, that's a whole lot of expense."

He nearly laughed out loud. What could it possibly cost to run a load of wash? A few dollars? "Yes, I'm sure it is a whole lot of expense, as you say."

She gave him a curious look. Damn. He'd been too formal. He needed to loosen up. Become more of a jeans guy. Kane cleared his throat and tried again. "Yeah, I'd rather not spend the cash, if I can help it. You know, watching the budget on vacation, and all."

"I can wash your shirt for you."

"Oh no, really, you don't have to."

"It's no trouble. How many shirts could you have brought with you for a vacation? You probably need this one, right?"

He didn't. How could he tell her he had dozens and

dozens exactly like this back home? That a shirt like this didn't come from any old corner discount store, but from a tailor Kane had known since he took his first steps? That he could flip out his cell phone and have three more custom made and in his hands in a matter of a day? "You're right," he lied. "I only have a couple of shirts with me."

"Then come on over to my house, and we'll take care of that mess."

Go over to her house. Alone. And do some laundry? Heck, right now he'd probably follow her to sort recyclables. "Sure, sounds good."

But as they got up and tossed their trash away, Kane realized every time he tried to untangle himself from his life, all he was doing was creating even more of what he already had on his hands.

A mess.

What had seemed like a good idea at the time had suddenly turned into one very bad idea. Susannah stood in the laundry room, a bottle of detergent in her hands, and tried really hard not to stare at Kane Lennox's bare chest.

The man could have been a commercial for weight machines. Or cologne. Or, heck, bottled sex appeal. Broad shoulders framed a well-defined chest, with a true washboard abdomen. What kind of workout did the guy do? Whatever his regimen, he'd make millions selling the steps to that physique.

She knew a few women who'd pay just to touch him. Present company not included. Of course.

Uh-huh. Boy, she could barely even lie to herself.

"Do you need to wash anything else? Or just my shirt?" Kane asked.

Damn. He'd caught her staring. "Just a few things," she

said, then turned back to the washer, twisting the dial until water started filling the tub. She dropped his oxford inside, added a few other items from a nearby basket, then closed the lid.

"I'm no expert at this, but don't you need some kind of soap, too?" He gestured toward the plastic bottle still in her grasp.

Heat filled her face. If Susannah could have crawled into the washing machine herself, she would have. "I, uh, forgot." She unscrewed the cap on the detergent and measured the right amount of liquid before adding it to the already churning water.

That's what she got for staring at the man's naked chest. No more doing that. Uh-huh. Easier said than done while he was all exposed like that.

"Do you want to borrow one of Paul's shirts? I'm sure he's left one or two clean ones behind. He's always doing his laundry over here. At least until yours is dry?"

"Nothing against Paul, but he's a foot shorter and fifty pounds lighter than me." Kane grinned. "I don't think anything he owns will fit."

Susannah's gaze drifted back to Kane's bare chest. He had one thing right. He definitely had more build than Paul. "Won't you be...cold?"

The grin quirked up higher on one side. "Not if you aren't."

The temperature between them arced upward, spiking three degrees, five, ten. Susannah took a step back, and bumped into the stainless steel machine. She slid to the right, but there was nowhere to go in the small room. No way to insert any distance between herself and Kane. No way to lower the charge. "Would you like some... coffee?"

He gestured toward the churning appliance. "It appears I'm your hostage, for a while, at least. Do with me what you will."

Temptation curled a tight grip around her. She wanted to kiss him—and wanted to run. Susannah hurried out of the laundry room and down the hall to the kitchen. "Decaf okay?" Because she definitely didn't need the extra stimulant of caffeine.

"Fine with me."

She skidded to a halt on the vinyl tile. New dirty dishes littered the kitchen countertops. Already? When did Jackie and Paul have time to make these kinds of messes?

Susannah knew the answer. Friends stopped by the house as frequently as birds landing on telephone lines. Like their hosts, every guest helped themselves to food and silverware, but did little more than leave the mess behind, as if some troop of elves was going to whisk it away while they were watching the latest blockbuster movie. A half-empty bag of chips sat on the table, surrounded by crumpled dirty napkins and a stack of used paper plates. There were empty soda cans, beer bottles and pizza boxes, and a nearly empty container of mint chocolate chip ice cream melting onto the kitchen table.

Insensitive. Rude. And embarrassing. Before she could pray Kane would get derailed by a sidestep into the living room, he entered the kitchen. And didn't say a word, which said ten times more than if he'd asked her what human tornado had just run through the twelve-by-fourteen room.

Susannah's face heated. "It doesn't always look like a frat house around here," she said, grabbing several of the dirty dishes on her way to the sink. She loaded them into the sink, then started running water while she loaded the coffeepot. Though what she'd said wasn't true, she still felt compelled to defend her sister and future brother-in-law's slovenly habits. Irritation rose in her chest at the renewed mess, but she tamped it down. A few more days, that was all, and then she'd be gone, and they'd be doing their own dishes.

"I'm not complaining," Kane said, but she could see shock in every inch of his face. Clearly the man lived in neater conditions than this. He moved to sit down at the table, found a stack of newspapers from that afternoon in the chair and picked them up, then stood there, as if he'd never seen a pile like that before and hadn't the foggiest idea what to do with them.

"Let me get those," Susannah said, grabbing the papers from him. She dumped the sheets into the recycle bin, then began gathering the trash and tossed it away.

Kane lowered himself into the seat, with all the care of someone placing a delicate vase on an earthquake fault. "So you, uh, live here, with your sister?"

"And Paul, even though he doesn't technically live here, he's here so much, he might as well, too. But I'll only be here for a little while longer." She bustled around the kitchen, working on the trash and the dishes in a two-prong approach. Take the pizza box to the trashcan, on the way back stop for the glasses, drop some of the dishes into the sink. Repeat the process over and over. Rover settled on a small carpet by the back door, curling himself into a furry ball before falling asleep.

"You're moving out, after the wedding?"

"Yes."

"And buying your own house?"

She laughed. "That's not in my budget, no. Dog washing doesn't pay *that* well."

"You must have a five-year plan."

She turned around to face him, putting her back to the sink. "Five-year plan? I'm just trying to get through this wedding, then get the hell out of this town for a little while before I have to return to the real world. Then I'll worry about the rest."

"That's hardly a smart strategy."

"Excuse me? You don't know me. Why do you think you can tell me how to live my life?"

"I…" He paused. "I don't. You're right. It's a bad habit of mine."

"Well, break it." She pivoted back to the dishes and began filling the sink. Regret washed over her. She'd jumped on Kane—and she rarely did that to people. He was merely being honest, and that was the one trait she valued most in others. "I'm sorry. I'm a little tense, because there's been so much going on around here lately."

"And I was completely out of line. I guess I'm just used to being in charge." He put out his hand. "Truce?"

When Susannah shook Kane's hand, electric heat jolted her senses. She broke away and returned to the sink. "If you're hungry, we can, ah, make some sandwiches."

"That would be great."

"Do you mind starting them? Then I can get these dishes out of the way." *And I can avoid looking at your bare chest, and touching you and thinking about touching you. All bad ideas, because I am totally not getting into a relationship right now.* "I know that's breaking all the rules of Hostess 101, but I can't stand a full sink." She shot him a smile, one she hoped covered every one of her traitorous thoughts.

"Sure." Kane rose, and Susannah tore her gaze away from his bare chest for the fortieth time. "Uh…where do you want me to start?"

With me. Just one kiss. Then—

"The fridge. There's ham and cheese in there. We could grill the bread. If you like. Or—" she glanced again at him and her thoughts raced one more time around the hormonal track "—not."

"Okay."

A note of doubt rose in his voice, but when Susannah looked back, Kane was in the refrigerator, searching for the ingredients. And searching some more. And some more. "Try the door," she said. "In the little compartment, above the eggs."

He lifted the clear lid, then pulled out the packaged American cheese slices. "*This* is cheese? In these little wrappers?"

She laughed. "Haven't you had American cheese before?"

He held the package in his hand, flipping it back to front, then front again, his nose wrinkling up with an expression that said he had about as much familiarity with the bright yellow slices as he did with Martians. "Oh, yeah. Uh, maybe."

Who had never tasted American cheese? Before she could puzzle over Kane's reaction, he was back in the fridge. "Where did you say I'd find the ham?"

"In the slim drawer, the center one."

He rummaged some more, then swung around, a second package in his opposite hand. Susannah paused, nearly losing the plate from her soapy grip. If there was a sexier sight than a half naked man holding sandwich fixings, she had yet to see it.

"Is this what you were talking about?"

"Uh…yeah," she said.

"*This* is *ham*." A statement, more than a question. Again, he gave the prepackaged ingredients a curious once-over. "From a deli?"

Susannah laughed. "From a grocery store. I assure you, it's good to eat. Bread's in the breadbox." When Kane remained rooted to the spot, she gave him a helpful point in the right direction. "Mayo's in the fridge, if you want that, on the door. Mustard's right beside it. And butter knives are in the drawer by my hip." She shifted to the right. Kane's gaze followed the movement, hunger darkening his cobalt eyes.

A shiver chased up her spine. So she wasn't the only one with a little heightened awareness.

The glass in her fingers slipped beneath the water, bouncing against the stainless steel sink. Susannah concentrated again on her work, instead of on Kane. He'd be gone in a few days, and so would she. Sharing anything more than a sandwich with him would be foolish.

Crazy.

Irresponsible.

And if there was one word no one would ever find on Susannah Wilson's personal résumé, it was *irresponsible*.

The glass joined plates in the strainer, followed by silverware. Soon the sink began to empty out and the pile of dirty dishes disappeared. She glanced over at Kane, expecting to see a stack of sandwiches and finding instead—

A man who looked lost.

"Need some help?"

"Uh…" Kane held the butter knife in an *en garde* position over the bread and condiments, then lowered it again. "Yeah."

Susannah drained the sink, dried her hands, then moved beside him. "Having trouble deciding between mustard and mayo or something?"

He looked down at the bright yellow bottle of mustard. "I'm just used to a…different kind."

"Sorry. This is all I had. I might have some honey mustard or maybe some Dijon in the cabinet, if you want me to look."

"No, no, I'm fine." He unscrewed the mayonnaise jar, dipped the knife into the container, then slapped a glob of the white stuff onto a slice of wheat.

"You really like your mayonnaise."

"Is that too much?" He stepped back, appraised his work. "It looks like a science experiment gone awry, doesn't it?"

"Hey, it's your sandwich."

"Cooking is not exactly my forte." He held the knife out to her. "You want to take over?"

"I think I better. I can already feel my cholesterol jumping off the charts." She shot him a grin, then, in the space of a few seconds, had two ham and cheese sandwiches assembled and placed on paper plates. She added fresh mugs of coffee, then gestured toward the kitchen table. "We can eat here, or take it outside. Rover might prefer the latter."

"Outside," Kane said. "On this trip, I want to spend as much time outdoors as I can. I spend way too many hours in an office."

An office. He'd said jewelry store earlier. Maybe Kane was a manager, or maybe she was getting too hung up on details. Susannah wanted to ask, then remembered their "Just Kane" and "Just Susannah" pact, and didn't say a word.

After switching the laundry to the dryer, Susannah led him through the kitchen and out to the deck, Rover bringing up the rear. As soon as they hit the backyard, Rover's little legs were in motion, carrying him around the grassy space, from tree to shrub, one massive scent investigation. "He's having a great time."

"I can already attest to the front yard's attributes. I'll let Rover give you the doggy thumbs-up on the back. Or is it paws-up?" Kane gave her a teasing smile.

She sat in a deck chair, easing into the thick cushion, the sandwich forgotten. For now, there was a gorgeous man smiling at her, and she was going to enjoy that. "Thanks again for your help today. I never would have finished without you."

"It was my pleasure. And believe me, I understand having too much on your plate."

Before Susannah could answer him, Kane's cell phone started chirping. Rover barked, startled by the sound, and started running in a circle. Susannah rose, helping to calm the dog. "I don't think they're going to give up unless you answer that."

"You're probably right." Kane flipped out the cell, then huffed a hello into the receiver.

Rover made a barking beeline for a squirrel running across the back of the yard. Susannah followed him, catching snippets of Kane's conversation as she went by, noting the lines of frustration in his face. Because of the dog? Or the caller?

"Leonard, I told you not to call me." Kane paused. "I know you're nervous about this deal, but you and Sawyer can handle it. A week won't make any difference. Might even bring the price down." Another pause. The lines deepened in Kane's forehead and he turned, pacing a tight circle on the deck. "No. Don't tell them a damned thing, Leonard. I'll be back on Monday, and not a minute sooner."

Susannah headed inside with the dog, to retrieve Kane's shirt from the dryer. By the time she returned to the backyard, Kane was tucking the phone away. "I'm sorry you had to step in and take over with the dog. But I appreciate it." He took the shirt from her and began putting it back on, much to her disappointment. "Thanks for washing this. It looks like new again."

"No problem." Though a large part of her wished the washer had messed up and either shrunk or ruined the shirt so she could have gotten that fabulous male view for a while longer. She gestured toward the cell. "Work issues?"

A muscle in his jaw twitched. The easygoing friendliness from earlier had disappeared and an icy tension descended over Kane. "Something like that."

"You're not the type of guy who answers a question with a paragraph, are you?" Susannah fell into step beside him as they crossed the yard. Rover found a stick, picked it up and brought it with him, ever hopeful. Kane ignored the offered game of fetch. What had that Leonard wanted that had made Kane turn on and off like a switch?

"Thanks for the sandwich, but I better get back to my cabin. Come on, Rover, time to go." He fished his keys out of his pocket, thumbed the remote on his rental car and waited for the answering beep.

"You're leaving?"

"I have…a mess I have to clean up. It seems it wasn't as easy to take a break from my life as I expected." He let out a sigh. "I don't know why I thought it would be."

Kane placed a hand on the gate of her fence, then turned back to face Susannah. A flicker of regret filled his eyes, then disappeared, gone as fast as a cloud on a sunny day.

Before she could read anything more, he pushed through the gate, climbed in his car and drove away, a man who clearly had a lot of secrets. And wasn't sharing any of them.

CHAPTER SIX

How did he get roped into these things? All his life, Kane Lennox had delegated. Prioritized. Said no to timewasters. He opened his mouth to do exactly that when Paul beat him to the punch.

"Man, I hate to even ask you for a favor," Paul said, grinning. "But you know I will."

They sat in Flanagan's Pub in downtown Chapel Ridge—or what passed for downtown, considering it was nothing more than a couple of streetlights. The shamrock-decorated barroom played country music, served peanuts and reminded Kane of the ones he and Paul had frequented years ago. The easy camaraderie the two men had had in college had been restored, as if not a moment had passed since graduation. Over a couple of beers, Kane had caught up on Paul's life, his job teaching history to high schoolers, his parents moving to Florida last year—just about everything.

When it came to his own life, Kane remained close-mouthed. What could he say, really? Life's the same. Still rich. Still overworked. No one wanted to hear those complaints.

"When was the last time you took a vacation, anyway?"

Paul asked. "I mean, with your bank account, you must go on some pretty rockin' trips."

"This is my first."

"First?" Paul let out a curse of disbelief. "Dude, in case you didn't notice, you could *buy* the island. You don't even have to rent a room there."

Kane chuckled. "The one thing I can't buy is time. Every year, I'd plan a vacation, and then a crisis would arise. My father or someone at the company would need me. And with my father…" He let out a breath. "It was complicated. I'd stay, you know, because I'd keep hoping that this time if I stepped up and played the hero for the company, he'd beat the drum and say, 'Hey, this is my son, would you look at him?' But he never did. Still, like an idiot, I kept on making those sacrifices. After a while, I just stopped planning trips. My assistant ended up taking most of them, anyway."

"That's sad, Kane. Totally sad."

He shrugged. "I'm here now. I got tired of beating a dead issue. When you called, it was like a lightbulb went off, and I said to hell with it all, walked out that door and came. Worked out great for both of us."

"And I totally appreciate it, too. I even get the whole mojito thing."

"Mojito?" Kane puzzled the word around. "Do you mean incognito?"

"Yeah, that's what I said. And I'm all for it, I mean, I've done the same thing a couple times."

"You have." It wasn't a question, but Kane put the words out there all the same.

Paul nodded, then took a long gulp of beer. "There was this time, back before I met Jackie, so, it was…well, in my wilder days. You remember those, don't you, Kane?"

A grin crossed Kane's face. "Barely."

"I know, you were a Lennox. And a Lennox doesn't party." Paul leaned over, lowering his beer and his voice. "Or at least, he doesn't if Charles the butler's watching."

"But when the butler's sleeping…" Kane added sotto voce, smiling at the shared memory of sneaking out of the dorm rooms with Paul, the only guy on campus who hadn't treated him like a leper because he'd arrived at Northwestern in a limo, and then later, with a butler for a roommate "…that's when the fun can start."

Paul clinked his bottle against Kane's. "You know it, buddy. God, there are days when I really miss those years."

"You and me both," Kane said, taking a deep pull off the bottle, the feel of the glass against his lips foreign to him. Ten years had passed since he'd drunk straight from a bottle, and even then he'd only been able to do it when Charles hadn't been around.

Because a Lennox never acted common.

A Lennox never raised his voice.

A Lennox never created a scene.

And most of all, a Lennox never did anything that would end up in the papers—except be born, get married and die. And all three of those things better be done in a dignified manner, by God, or he'd find himself on the other side of the Lennox name faster than a dog that had peed on the Aubusson carpet.

But in those months before his father had sicced Charles on him, Kane and Paul had had fun. Kane would always be grateful to Paul for that—and for the nights they had snuck out on the eagle-eyed Charles because it had provided much-needed sanity and normalcy in a life as constricting as a straitjacket.

Paul picked a few peanuts out of the small wooden bowl

on the bar, popped them into his mouth, chewed and swallowed. "So, have you told Susannah who you are?"

"No. And I'm not going to."

Paul lowered his voice. "No one knows who you are? How is that possible?"

"Nobody knows who *runs* a company, Paul. They see the ads for Lennox Gems, sure, but it doesn't say CEO Kane Lennox at the bottom or anything. As long as my father doesn't start some media frenzy, I'm fine. And I don't want to tell Susannah or anyone else who I am because—" Kane toyed with his beer bottle "—I'm tired of people who look at me as a dollar bill first and a human being second."

"Your secret's safe with me, Kane. I owe you." Paul clapped him on the back.

"You owe *me?* For what?"

"You were my sanity for getting through college, too. My old man, he thought a history degree was a waste of time. A waste of my football scholarship to Northwestern." Paul spun the bottle on the bar. "Who was I kidding, though? I was never going to play pro ball. You gotta get fairy dust for that kind of career. I needed a real plan. A real job. But my old man, he wanted the NFL or nothing. You…you understood, Kane. And I don't know if I ever told you how much that meant to me."

Kane shrugged. "You didn't have to."

"Yeah." Paul nodded, in the near silent communication of men. Then he grinned and tapped his beer bottle against Kane's. "If Susannah tries to kill me for keeping a secret from her and her sister, you will hire me a bodyguard, won't you?"

"Of course."

"Good." He unearthed some cashews this time. "And you sure you don't mind doing this favor for me tonight?

It won't be as fun as some of our midnight raids on the women's dorm rooms, but it won't be horrible, either."

"Now I know why you never went into sales," Kane deadpanned.

Paul chuckled. "Susannah's my sister-in-law, Kane. She's not a five-year-old dented Caddy I'm trying to unload. She's…nice."

"I know she is." Very nice, indeed. But Kane kept those thoughts to himself. If he spoke them aloud, Paul would be running a matchmaker service right in Flanagan's. What Paul wouldn't understand was why Kane and Susannah would be wrong for each other in the long run.

Susannah Wilson was the kind of woman men had permanent thoughts about. The kind of woman a man married. And the exact kind of woman—

His father would ship off to Europe for being "unacceptable" as a Lennox family addition.

Paul dug through the bowl of nuts again. "Damn. All the cashews are gone. And the peanuts. Larry, are you getting cheap on the nut mix again?"

"No, you're just getting greedy," the bartender said, giving Paul a good-natured grin.

"Next he'll be serving popcorn and calling it a meal." Paul pushed the bowl away, then turned back to Kane and gestured over his shoulder after the stout bartender had crossed to the opposite end. "He's a good guy, Larry is, but he's had a hard time. I went to school with him."

"What do you mean, hard time?"

"His kid's got leukemia." Paul shook his head. "'Bout breaks my heart. But Larry, you'd never know it. He's got a smile for everyone who comes in here. The town threw him a benefit a few months ago, to raise some money for the medical bills. That's what small towns are like, Kane. They're like families, only bigger."

"And without the politics."

Paul chuckled. "Trust me, small towns still have politics. Speaking of weird things in small towns, don't go running around barefoot on the lawn anymore, either. What was that about, anyway?"

"My feet were hot."

Okay, that had to be the lamest excuse known to man, but Kane wasn't going to get all honest with Paul. He had no desire to tell another guy—good friend or not—that he had had this sudden urge to feel spring grass beneath his toes. Paul would label him crazy for sure.

Paul must have agreed with the lame part because he laughed, then shook his head. "Yeah. Whatever floats your boat. But don't do it again. You'll scare the neighbors."

Kane nodded. "Are you sure Susannah wants to go out with me?"

"Let me put it this way. Jackie wants to be alone with me. Susannah lives with us, and I know for a fact she doesn't have any plans for tonight, so she should be easy to persuade. Either way, we're desperate, so if you don't get Susannah out of the house…" He put up his hands.

"You're getting married in three days, Paul."

"In all the years you've known me, have you ever called me a patient man?" Paul tipped the beer to emphasize his point. "Exactly. Nothing against Susannah, but Jackie and I just want a night alone. I need to talk to Jackie anyway. She's running through our wedding budget like it's Halloween candy. I love her, but she's got no concept of money, or taking things easy. But talking to Jackie requires a little…buttering up, if you know what I mean." Paul grinned. "So do me a favor, Kane, take Susannah out. Let her show you the sights."

Kane laughed. "In Chapel Ridge? That'll take, what, ten minutes?"

Paul rose and clapped him on the back. "Improvise, my friend. If I remember right, that was your *real* major in college. Especially when it came to fooling the butler into thinking you were behaving."

"Fishing. You want to take me fishing." Susannah stared at Kane Lennox, sure she had heard him wrong. Of all the vacationers she had met, this man looked the least like a fisherman. Especially wearing those designer shoes and pressed jeans. Granted, he'd exchanged his button-down shirts for a T-shirt and a green Chapel Ridge sweatshirt, but he still had that dressed-up air about him, despite the more casual attire.

Nevertheless, Kane was well stocked with fishing accessories. He held out a pole to her, then raised a plastic tackle box into view. "It's always more fun with two, don't you agree?"

"What about Paul? He's your best friend, isn't he? And fishing is a guy thing."

"Paul has…plans."

Susannah shot a glance at her future brother-in-law. He spread his palms up and gave her a blank look of innocence. "Plans. Sorry."

Plans? She couldn't remember Jackie mentioning anything. "Wha—"

Then over her shoulder, she caught a glimpse of Jackie, setting out a trio of candles on the dining room table. Jackie, wearing a black skirt, and a sexy red V-neck shirt, her hair long and curled.

Date hair. Date clothes. Date candles.

The lightbulb burst in Susannah's brain. Her face

heated, and she took a step back. "Oh. Those plans. Uh…I should…uh…"

"Fish," Kane finished, filling her hand with the pole and giving her a grin. "You should go fishing. With me."

"Or you can stay with us," Jackie said, with all the conviction of a low-willpower dieter in a cookie factory. "Paul and I were just going to rent a movie and—"

"Kane's *really* looking for a fishing partner," Paul cut in, taking Jackie's hand and giving it a squeeze. "You know how it is, Suzie-Q, when you go on vacation, and you want to do stuff, but you don't really know anyone to do anything with."

No, she didn't, she wanted to tell them. Because she had never been on vacation. Had never left this town. Instead, she pasted on a smile, gave the fishing pole a little shake, and grabbed her denim jacket. "Sorry I'll miss the movie," she said. "Save me some popcorn."

"Before you poke my eye out," Kane said, slipping into the driver's seat of his rental car, opposite Susannah, "let me take this and—" He took the fishing pole, rolled down the window and threw it onto the ground.

"What are you doing?"

"Disarming you. Before you blame me for what happened back there. Or…let me take all the blame, anyway."

She crossed her arms over her chest. "Were you in on the plan?"

"Well…" He swallowed. "Maybe a little. But I had no idea they were going to shove you out the door like a—"

"Houseguest who had overstayed his welcome? Like a repo man who showed up to take away the family's minivan just before the soccer playoffs? Like—"

He put up his hands. "Truce. I get the hint. And I'm sorry."

Susannah sank further into the seat. "Apparently it's me who can't get the hint."

He started the car and put it into gear, pulling away from Jackie and Paul's house. Rover settled down in the backseat, clearly content to go for a ride in the car. "Don't feel bad. Paul and Jackie are just too focused on their own merger to realize the collateral damage they're leaving in their wake."

"Either way, I won't be here to be caught in the ripples anymore."

He glanced over at her. "Where are you going?"

"Travel, see the world. As soon as the wedding's over. I'm closing my shop and getting out of town for a few weeks."

"Really? Why?"

"Because I want more. I want that life. The life everyone else seems to have and I seem to have missed." She traced a pattern along the window.

He let out a little laugh.

"What?"

"Nothing."

"You find my idea funny."

"No. Just…ironic." He took a left, not going anywhere in particular that Susannah could tell. They certainly weren't going fishing, since the fishing pole was back on Jackie's lawn.

"How so?"

"Some people," he began, seeming to choose his words carefully as he made yet another turn, "seek out the opposite of what you are looking for. They find the bright lights and big city aren't all they're purported to be, and instead, they reach for the solitude of the very life you already have."

Susannah shook her head. "I can't imagine why. There's nothing here that I want."

"Maybe so. For you." He turned down one more road, then stopped the car. They had, after all, stopped by the far end of Lake Everett. A few feet away, the still waters glistened under the moonlight, dark and tranquil, holding their secrets in an almost ebony peace. Far across the lake, the lights of the hotel twinkled, flanked by the flicker of the occasional firepit from the cabins.

"I thought we weren't going fishing."

"We aren't. But unless you have another plan, we still can't go back to your house, and I didn't think you wanted to be…well, alone in my cabin. And almost everything else in this town seems to shut down after five."

"Exactly why I want to leave and eventually move away, if I can take my business elsewhere."

Kane turned the car off and pocketed the keys, then grabbed a black leather jacket from the backseat. "Come on, let's take a walk."

Alone with Kane. In the dark. Temptation curled its grip around Susannah.

She wanted to resist. Knew she should. She had no time for a man in her life, no room for a relationship, especially one with someone who would be gone soon. "I should probably go to work. Get some paperwork done—"

He reached out and clasped her hand, cutting off her words and, with the electricity in his touch, her breath. "There's always going to be time for work. Believe me. But there won't always be a night as beautiful as this. Take it from someone who knows."

Then he got out of the car and came around to her side, opening her door before she could disagree. Rover clambered over the seat and leapt out of the car, bounding toward the lake.

Susannah stopped, drinking in the view. How long had

it been since she'd taken the time to admire the lake at night? "It's like diamonds," Susannah said softly. "The moonlight, on the lake."

"I agree," Kane said. "Did you know, like snowflakes, no two diamonds are alike? The oldest diamond is billions of years old, yet we've only been mining them for a couple thousand years."

"Wow. I didn't realize that." She followed him down the grassy path to the lake, reaching out to steady herself with a tree. Rover scrambled along with them, stopping every few seconds to unearth a new treasure, from pinecones to rocks.

"They're amazing gems, diamonds are, and one of my favorites. Cutting and polishing a stone can take away as much as half of its size. It takes a true artisan to be able to see a raw diamond and realize its potential." Kane bent over, picked up a handful of rocks and jingled them in his palm. Beneath the stars, strains of quartz glinted.

She ran a finger over the marbled seam of the largest rock, then drew back. "How do they know what shape to cut the diamond in?"

"Ah, that's where skill comes in." Kane dropped the rocks to the ground, then dusted his palms together. Rover headed off to nose at the edge of the lake, darting into the water, then back out, as if playing a game with the lapping waves. "Not just anyone can be a diamond cutter and polisher. It's a skill that's passed down from generation to generation. Fathers teach sons, grandfathers teach their grandsons."

"No mothers teaching daughters?" She grinned.

"Some. But mostly, it's about getting quiet with the stone. Looking at it, hearing what shape it should be, and being true to the stone's nature before you lay a single tool against it."

Susannah bent down, grabbed a thick rock that had likely sat at the edge of this lake since this beginning of time, and hefted it in her palm, as if it were a rare gem. "Everyone's always looking to create the next Hope diamond, is that it?"

"No, not really. What gets jewelers and people who work with gems excited is finding that next rare jewel. Or seeing the one no one else has ever seen. A red diamond, for instance, is the rarest of all. And then the public will create a demand for something like chocolate diamonds, which are diamonds with brownish tones. Years ago, no one wanted them. Now, they're the next hot thing."

Susannah replaced the rock, then rose, brushing her palms off on her jeans. "Working in a jewelry store must be romantic." She hugged her arms around her chest, a slight barrier against the cool evening breeze. Her denim jacket was too light for the midspring weather and she found herself wishing she'd dressed warmer.

He laughed. "Romantic?"

"All those couples coming in, picking out engagement rings. All those people thinking forever is just a gold band away."

Kane took off his leather jacket and draped it over her shoulders, settling his palms on her for just a second, as if cementing the coat in place. She leaned into his touch, then drifted away before shooting him a smile of gratitude. She couldn't remember the last time a man had done something so chivalrous—without being prompted.

"You sound mildly against the prospect of marriage," Kane said.

"For me, not as a rule for everyone."

"Because?"

"Because I think that not everyone ends up with the fairy tale. That's all."

"And because you have other plans."

"Exactly."

They began walking the perimeter of the lake, a slow stroll, allowing the spaniel to continue his playful game with the water's edge.

"So what would you do if you suddenly met Mr. Right? Say, while you're hiking across the Alps or touring Big Ben?"

She laughed. "The chances of that are pretty slim."

"Perhaps."

He stopped, then picked up a rock and skipped it across the serene water's surface. It bounced twice before sinking to the bottom. "That's exactly why I never tried out for the baseball team."

"You need a flatter stone," Susannah said. "That one was too round."

She bent, searching in the earth for the right rock, then when she found one, stood and put her palm out flat to show Kane. "Try this one."

"Show me."

"Okay. But I'll warn you, you're dealing with a pro here."

She turned slightly, then drew her arm back, and in one fluid movement, let the rock go. It skipped five times, bouncing in lower and lower arcs, before slipping beneath the inky water.

"Wow. You're really good at that."

She shrugged. "I told you so."

"I mean it. How did you get so adept at stone skipping?"

"I used to have a lot of time on my hands after school. Waiting on Jackie to catch up, while we were walking home."

"Was she just a slow walker?"

"No. She was what you call a social butterfly. Still is. She had to stop and say hello to everyone she saw. Instead of waiting like a third wheel, I'd go do my own thing and she knew I'd be here at the lake. I'd skip stones or climb trees or do any of the tomboyish things that my sister thought were the kiss of death."

"Kiss of death?"

"For a respectable social life." Susannah laughed. "Maybe she was right. After all, she's the one who's getting married. And I'm the one…still skipping rocks."

Kane slipped both his hands into Susannah's and turned her in the dark to face him. Beneath the silvery beams of the moon, her countenance glowed with a faint shimmer, bouncing off her eyes, her lips. She'd been wrong. It wasn't the lake that glittered with diamonds, it was Susannah. Her eyes. Her hair. Everything about her. He captured her jaw, turned her mouth up to meet his, intending only to catch her attention, but instead finding he had caught himself in the spell ten times more.

"You're much more than that, Susannah. You're…so different from anyone I've ever met."

"So plain, you mean. So—"

"So unique." His thumb caressed a lazy circle along her jawline, silky peach skin working almost like a balm to his tough exterior. To a man who had left New York jaded, overworked, sure there was no one left in the world who possessed an innocent bone in their body, she brought a sense of peace, of hope, to Kane's soul.

Susannah Wilson seemed to be the very embodiment of what women should be. Nurturing. Unpretentious. And yet, at the same time, a challenge.

"Listen, you don't have to butter me up," she said, "just because you're the best man. I'm not feeling left out of the wedding or anything like that. I know Paul and Jackie probably sold you some kind of sob story about the poor eldest sister, the spinster, as if God forbid that's some kind of crime around here. In a small town, it's like a disease not to be married. But I'm—"

"You talk too much," he said, silencing her speech with a finger to her lips.

"I—"

"I can see it'll take a lot more to shut you up," he said, teasing. Then he leaned forward and did what he'd wanted to do nearly from the moment he'd met Susannah.

He kissed her.

At first, she held her ground, unyielding to his touch, then finally she softened against him by degrees—her lips, her face, her touch. She leaned into his body, her hands ranging up his back, reaching higher, until she had him pulled against her, tight, firm.

And Kane's world exploded.

Damn. He had kissed women. Dozens of them. Women who purred against him. Women who stood still as statues. Women who made it their life's mission to cater to his every need. But never had he kissed a woman who poured herself so wholeheartedly into something so simple as a kiss.

Susannah tasted of the bitterness of coffee, mixed with the sweetness of cookies. The air held the vanilla and citrus notes of her perfume, the wave of her body heat.

His grip tightened around her, desire singing its siren song through his veins, pounding in his head. He tangled his hands in her hair, letting the silky strands slip through his fingers like a rainstorm. Knowing that for as long as he lived, this would be a kiss as unforgettable as his first.

Finally, Susannah stepped back, out of his embrace. "What...what was that?"

He grinned. "If I have to tell you, then maybe you want to repeat health class."

She swatted him gently on the shoulder. "That wasn't what I meant and you know it. Why did you kiss me?"

"Because I wanted you. Simple as that."

"I don't want a relationship."

"Did I say I did?"

"But…" Confusion warred in her gaze. "Why kiss me then?"

"Does every kiss have to lead to a walk down the aisle with you?"

She laughed. "You're in a small Indiana town. Things out here are different. We don't do too many things halfway."

He reached out and trailed a finger down her cheek, watched her sharp inhale of breath, as an echoing roar ran through his chest. "Maybe it's time you did, Suzie-Q."

CHAPTER SEVEN

THE world had turned inside-out, upside-down and sideways.

Why did Kane Lennox have to go and kiss her? Just when Susannah thought she had everything on an even keel, thought she had a plan for the days ahead, for her life—okay, maybe not her life, but at least for the next few weeks—he'd gone and added an X to an even equation. She didn't need a relationship, even a temporary one.

And she especially didn't need to be kissed by a man who made her wonder if she'd been missing out on something all her life, as if there was some great secret every other woman in the world had been holding tight—and she'd just now discovered.

Because, damn, that man could kiss.

Definitely better than her first boyfriend, Darryl Taylor. Ten times better than Tim Mills, her last boyfriend—and the one she'd dated the longest, for two years. Not that any of the men she'd dated had been bad or inattentive. Simply clearly lacking something in the experience department.

Except…more experience meant Kane had a lot of women to choose from. A lot of women in his dating past—who also must have had plenty of experience. If that was so, why would he want to date someone he'd met on vacation, a woman from a small Indiana town? Unless, as he'd said, all he wanted was a quick little fling?

Nothing more than kisses?

And did Susannah want the same thing?

"A penny for your thoughts." Kane slipped his hand into hers and began walking with her around the perimeter of the lake.

"Why are you here? Besides the wedding?"

"My job is stressful and I thought I could use a few days off. I haven't taken a vacation in...well, forever."

"Yeah, but why here? Chicago is only a few hours away. Detroit. Cincinnati. Heck, you could hop on a plane and be about anywhere but here."

"I live in a city. I wanted something different."

"And I live in the small town. I want the city. Guess we're the two proverbial mice."

"Or maybe, once you get to the big city, you'll find out that everything you ever wanted was here to begin with."

"Maybe once you spend more than a few hours here, you'll realize you were crazy for thinking there was anything more exciting than watching corn growing here."

He laughed, a deep, hearty sound that she couldn't help but echo. "Maybe."

Rover came charging up from the water's edge and ran a frenzied circle around their legs, then took off for the water again, as if trying to entice them to join him in his hunt for creatures at the lake's edge. Kane chuckled at the spaniel's antics. "Why don't you own a dog of your own?"

"I work with them all day, and that's enough for me. Plus, I want to travel, and it wouldn't be fair to the dog to just keep leaving him or her home, or boarded at a kennel. But I love dogs. They're my favorite animals in the world."

"Why? I mean, cats are cute, too, right?"

Susannah chuckled. "Yeah, I like cats, too. But there's something about dogs. You always know where you stand. They're honest. That's why I started working with them. There's none of that rubbish you get with people. Dogs are easy to read, easy to please, and they give back what they get. Honesty is important to me, and so I chose the most honest creatures on earth to be my coworkers, of sorts." She smiled.

"Maybe I should hire in a bunch of golden retrievers instead of stuffy executives."

Susannah laughed. "You might get better results. And even better, they work for biscuits."

They walked a while longer. Kane's hand captured Susannah's, as naturally as if they had always done this, always walked together. She held on to his palm, allowing herself to enjoy the little thrill that ran through her whenever Kane touched her. Out in the middle of the lake, a fish jumped, spoiling the serene surface. From far across the lake, someone turned on a stereo. With the clear night, the sounds of the song carried crisply on the air.

"Someone must have read my mind and added a little mood music," Kane said. "Would you like to dance?"

Susannah shook her head. "I have a lot of skills in life. Dancing is not one of them."

"You can't be the maid of honor and not dance."

She shrugged. "All eyes will be on Jackie, anyway."

He stopped walking, swung around her, captured her hands and then her gaze. Whenever Kane Lennox looked at her like that, a quiver began in Susannah's belly, and grew into a tingle that spread through her entire body. The breeze seemed to catch in the trees, the night birds stopped calling, the water stopped lapping at the shore. All Susannah heard was the rapid beat of her own heart, the heavy intake of her breaths. "I doubt that," he said. "Jackie may be the bride, but that doesn't automatically make her the most beautiful woman in the room."

Her face heated, and she broke eye contact with him. He didn't know the Wilson sisters. Jackie had always been the center of attention—and would be on Friday night, too. And that was fine with Susannah. Her turn was just around the corner.

Kane ran his thumbs over the back of her hands. She looked into his eyes, unable to forget his kiss from a moment ago, wishing he'd kiss her again, under this quiet veil of night.

"Dance with me, Susannah," Kane said softly, and she couldn't resist. Across the lake, the music had segued into something slow and easy, the bass throbbing out a beat as hot and heavy as their earlier kiss. "It seems they're playing our song."

"*This* is our song?"

Before she could protest, Kane slipped on arm around her waist, then put her hand into his opposite palm. She fit into his body with the ease of a missing puzzle piece, warmth seeking warmth, their legs stepping easily in rhythm, as if she'd done this all her life. "Any song that lets me do this with you is our song."

Oh, boy. She was in trouble.

Kane Lennox might be saying one thing—that he wanted nothing more than a few kisses, a turn or two around a dance floor, and she might be agreeing, but everything about this man, his charm, his easy way with her, sent Susannah's pulse racing into another stratosphere, and she simply couldn't imagine a quick entry and an even quicker exit.

Because she'd already begun to crave more. Another kiss. Another dance. And…

More? What if he stayed, beyond the wedding? What if she did? What if…

But no. That wouldn't happen. Because both of them had plans to leave town after the wedding. And this dance, these kisses, would be it. She could do this. She could have this moment of fun.

She closed her eyes and gave in to the music. To his touch. To the easy feel of his body against hers. The temptation for more rolled over her, whispering to her to abandon everything, just leave every responsible thought in her head behind.

"That's it," Kane said quietly, his voice as dark as the night. His hand inched up her back, helping her fit into his groove. "Just let yourself be, be one with the rhythm, with me."

From far off, a night bird called, his song an interruption to the one on the stereo. The sound brought her back to reality, reminding Susannah she could have a temporary reprieve from her responsibilities, but anything more was out of the question. She had a sister and a business to worry about. Until the wedding was over and until she was on that plane to Paris, her life really wasn't her own to have. Jackie still needed her—it was clear in all the bad decisions her sister kept making. And so did her business. Until then, a relationship could wait.

Susannah jerked back, out of Kane's arms. "I…I can't. This is…a bad idea."

"Dancing? Is a bad idea?"

She shook her head, trying to clear it. Of this man, of the possibilities he'd awakened. "This is more than dancing, and you know it."

"And what's so wrong with that?"

She turned away, and started heading back to his car. Rover

trotted alongside. "I really do have some work to get done tonight. If you don't mind dropping me off at the shop—"

"I do mind. You need to take time off as much as I do."

She whirled around. "Who asked you to drop into town and suddenly start telling me how to live my life? I got along just fine before you showed up."

He bit his lip and didn't say anything for a long moment. Then he nodded. "Okay. You win. I'll shut up and drive."

She grinned. "Now, that's got to be the best thing you've said all night."

He chuckled, the tense moment between them gone. "You really know how to romance a man, Susannah Wilson."

"See, that's the trouble, Kane," Susannah said with a sigh. This man had yet to hear her, really hear her. "I'm not trying to romance you. At all."

Even if a part of her kept saying otherwise.

Kane had lied.

Well, partly. He did drive Susannah to The Sudsy Dog. And he did drop her off. But he didn't go back to his cabin. He headed over to Flanagan's Pub, took a seat at the bar, and told himself several times he should go home, and instead lingered in downtown Chapel Ridge.

"So, are you a friend of Paul's?" the bartender asked.

Kane nodded. "In town for the wedding."

"He's a good guy. Him and Jackie both." The bartender put the glass he was drying on the shelf, then stuck out his hand. "Name's Larry."

"Kane." The two men shook. "I'm staying out at one of the lake cabins."

"Good fishing out there."

"So I hear."

Larry put a foot onto the stool beside him, his face drawing pensive. Behind him on the wall-mounted television, a sports commentator was droning on about spring training. "Yeah, I used to get out there all the time with my son. I miss it."

"Paul told me about him. I'm sorry to hear about all you've been through."

Larry shrugged. "It's been hard, but you know, living here makes it easier. Knock small towns all you want, but me and my wife, we got plenty of friends around here. Friends and family, they make 'bout anything easier to bear, don't you agree?"

"Yeah."

Though Kane's experience with either was slim, at least until he'd arrived in Chapel Ridge. Odd, in a matter of days, he felt closer to the residents of this town than he did to most of the executives at Lennox Gem Corporation.

"Anyway," Larry said, waving off the discussion, "you didn't come here to hear all about my problems. What can I get you?"

Kane was about to order a beer when he saw Susannah come out of her shop with three leashes in her hand—and three equally large dogs attached to the end of those leashes. "Uh, nothing, thanks. I just saw what I wanted outside."

Then he left, hurrying to his rental car to get Rover before heading over to Susannah.

"I thought you were going home," she said.

"And I thought you were going to do paperwork."

"This is one of the other parts of my job." She held up the leashes. "Walking the shelter dogs three times a day."

"Alone? At this time of night?"

Susannah laughed. "This is Chapel Ridge, Kane. Not the crime capital of the world. I'll be fine."

"If I promise not to tell you what to do with your life, how about you let me help you walk the dogs?"

She shouldn't let him. After all, "Just Kane" had this wall up she couldn't seem to see over. She understood him wanting a little privacy while he was on vacation, but she also had a nagging sense that he was hiding something—something big. And those red flags were becoming increasingly hard to ignore. "I have this under control."

"I'm sure you do. I'm simply sharing the burden." He reached over and took one of the leashes from her, brushing off her protests just as her heart did the same thing with her better judgment.

"You couldn't even walk a dog the other day."

"I'm a fast learner. Watch." He put a leash in each hand and strode forward. Except his plan didn't go the way he expected. Rover took one look at his new walking companion and let out a growl. The second dog answered with a growl of his own, and before Kane could say "stop," the two of them were circling each other with angry barks.

"I'll trade you." Susannah reached across him, took the leash of the black dog, walked that dog forward and away from Rover, then gave Kane the lead to a small white pooch instead. "You picked Dexter. He's a male, and when you put two males together—"

"They spend more time jockeying for position than getting any work done."

She laughed. "Yeah, that's pretty much it. So try this little girl." She handed him a terrier mix. "This is Sonya. She should get along fine with Rover. Just walk Rover on the far left, and I'll walk Dexter on my far right. And we'll all be one big happy family."

As soon as those words left her mouth, Susannah wanted to take them back. She barely knew this man. "One big happy family" did not describe them at all.

But Kane, if he'd noticed the phrase, didn't say anything. "The only problem is, we're outnumbered two to one, with the animals at a decided advantage."

Susannah grinned. "Do those odds scare you?"

"Nothing scares me."

"Oh, I bet some things do." She studied him, keeping her grip on the leashes firm, as they rounded a corner. She'd spent more time with Kane in the last couple of days than almost anyone besides Jackie, and yet, there were times when she felt as if she barely knew him. "Everyone is scared of something. What is it for you?"

He stopped walking and pivoted toward her. Beneath the streetlight, his every feature was outlined, his eyes seemed darker, more mysterious. "You want to know what scares me?"

Susannah nodded, mute. Her heart thudded in her chest.

Kane transferred both leashes to one hand, and reached up with the other to cup her jaw. Even as she told herself to hold back, to stay away, Susannah leaned into the touch, the warmth, the tenderness. "A woman who deserves so much more than I can give."

"I don't want anything, though."

Kane leaned in closer, his lips now a breath away. "Wanting and deserving are two different things. And what you deserve, Susannah Wilson, is the world. On a platter." Then he winnowed the gap, and kissed her again.

Her head spun, her pulse raced. She reached for him, but the dogs, impatient for their walk, tangled the leashes around Kane's and Susannah's legs and began vocalizing their desire to keep moving. She broke away from Kane.

Saved by the bark. "I think we better get going before our chaperones get too antsy."

"We probably should." He trailed a finger along her jaw. "But first, tell me, is there anything wrong with a little of that?"

"No," Susannah breathed.

"Then who says we can't do it again?" And he brushed his lips across hers before the dogs pulled him away.

And again, and again, a part of her demanded. But thankfully work—in the form of a bunch of canines—kept her on track.

Kane and Susannah headed down the sidewalk toward the town park. "We can have that," he said, referencing the kiss, "without a deep relationship. I'm only here for a few days, and so are you. I don't want to get into some big discussion about my life. Or my job. I just want to enjoy my time here, and my time with you. Is that so bad?"

Though it stung a little that Kane kept shutting the door every time Susannah knocked, she had to admit that he had a point. No getting too close, no ties in the end. "No, it's not."

Wasn't that what she wanted anyway? Nothing to bind her to this town, to her old life? So she could leave without remorse, begin a new life as soon as Jackie's wedding was over. It was exactly the type of relationship she told herself she should pursue, yet a part of herself kept rebelling, like a child who had spied the cookie jar and was now throwing a tantrum every time the treats came into view.

"Good. Because I need to ask you a favor."

"A favor?"

"I'm not quite getting what I need on this vacation and I think you're the only one who can provide what I want."

He stopped walking and turned to face her. "So I have a deal to offer you, Susannah. If you accept it, maybe we can both get what we want. What do you say?"

CHAPTER EIGHT

"You want me to do *what?*" Susannah stared at him. Around them, Chapel Ridge maintained its veil of silence, everyone asleep for the night, the businesses shut up, the residents tucked in their beds. As far as this corner of the world was concerned, the only people who existed were Susannah and Kane. They had waited to finish the conversation until the dogs were done with their walks and back in their kennels. Now, Susannah, Kane and Rover stood in the quiet night air outside the closed grooming salon.

"I want you to show me how to live like a normal person."

"Uh…is there a reason you don't know how?"

"I'm a…typical bachelor. Never really functioned on my own." He shifted from foot to foot, avoiding her gaze. "I want to experience life. But I'm not very good at it."

"As in…doing what?"

"Starting a fire, for one. So I don't freeze to death in that cabin. Last night was no fun, let me tell you. I'd make a really bad Eskimo." He smiled. "I want you to show me things like skipping stones. Maybe even cooking over an open flame."

"You're kidding."

"No, I'm not. And, I'm willing to pay you."

"*Pay* me?" The words rolled in her mind. Five minutes ago Kane had been talking about kissing her and, she'd thought, had been doing a very good job of trying to romance her.

Now he'd switched gears, and was offering to pay her to enhance his vacation experience. The contradictions in Kane Lennox ran deeper every second. Susannah had no doubts about his interest in her, but about his reasons for being in Chapel Ridge—beyond the wedding—she had several. About what he wanted beyond a few kisses, she had plenty more.

Could she put those doubts aside and trust him over the next few days? Without falling into the depths she saw in his eyes? Or would she be making the biggest mistake of her life by letting go of those tight reins she had on her emotions?

"I'll pay you more than enough money to make it worth your while, of course," Kane went on. "I realize this will interfere with your current job." He paused, seeming to run a mental calculator. "What do you make as a dog groomer? A hundred dollars an hour?"

"Maybe."

"I'll triple that. In exchange, you take the day off and show me what I want to see, teach me what I want to know."

Susannah nearly choked. Three hundred dollars an *hour?* More than two thousand dollars a *day?* Kane had to be joking…or insane. "Do you mean like a paid escort?"

"Well, not that kind, but yes."

"That's a ridiculous amount of money. No one pays that much for—" She stopped. "Are you rich or something?"

"I'm…I…I saved up a lot for this vacation."

"You saved up a lot for a vacation to *Chapel Ridge, Indiana?* And now you want to spend it on me? Specifically me teaching you how to do what ordinary people do every day for free?"

He didn't answer that question. "Are you turning me down?"

"No, but I'm assessing the wisdom of your offer. Not to mention your sanity in making it." And her sanity in agreeing. Every moment she spent with Kane wrapped her tighter in a spell she couldn't seem to break.

What did she have to worry about? This was all temporary. Saturday morning she'd be on a plane to the other side of the world. Surely that would be enough distance to forget him.

"Well, don't think so much. Just accept it." He reached into his back pocket and pulled out his wallet. "I assume cash is okay?"

Oh, my goodness. Kane was actually serious. When he handed Susannah a pile of hundred-dollar bills, her eyes widened. If she was frugal, she could envision these dollars becoming a jaunt over to London, maybe a quick side trip to Italy. The kernel of a savings account toward a trip to Germany or Mexico. "You carry around that much cash?"

"I'm not a fan of traveler's checks."

"Ever hear of credit cards?"

"Don't like those much, either. Cash is my way of doing business, at least on a personal level."

"Well, your ATM card must get a lot of wear." She stared at the bills in his hand, until he took her palm and placed them in hers, then she stared even more. "This is…this is way too much. You're insane."

"I only have a limited amount of time. I want my vacation to be the best it can be. And so far, all I've done is starve, freeze and find a dog I didn't want." He grinned. "The best time I had was with you. Every time I've been with you, Susannah, all I wanted to do was spend even more time with you. It didn't matter if we were washing a dog or throwing a fishing pole out the window." He took a step closer and tipped her jaw until her gaze met his. "Imagine how it would be if we had actual, planned fun together? If all I had to worry about, and all you had to worry about, was us being together? That, to me, would be a perfect vacation."

He saw Susannah's breath catch. When she looked at him like that, Kane could barely resist her. Every bone in his body longed to kiss her again, but he was afraid if he did, she really would think this offer was only for one thing— when it wasn't. Although, if he could kiss her a dozen more times over the next few days, he wouldn't complain.

"I suppose—" she fingered the hundreds "—I could have Tess take on a few extra appointments for me."

"And what about your sister's wedding plans?"

A smile crossed Susannah's face, a smile so wide it could have rivaled the sun's. And for the first time since Kane had made the crazy offer, he knew he had done the right thing.

"I think Jackie can handle her own wedding just fine, at least for a few hours a day. Apparently I have a new job."

Susannah had done some oddball things to fund her dream, but this took the cake. "You really want to do this?"

"Absolutely."

"Okay. It's your money." She handed him the shovel. "About here should be good."

He grinned, then pushed on the metal edge with his boot. The spade sank into the earth, turning up a chunk of dark brown sod. When it did, a trio of earthworms came squirming out of the ground. Rover took one look at them, let out a yelp and darted off. "Success!"

Susannah laughed. Kane Lennox made the oddest study

in contradictions in his perfect jeans and second, new, casual shirt, along with a pair of new boots Susannah had insisted he buy at the local hunter supply shop, coupled with his cocktail party mannerisms. All of them forgotten when he'd dug up a pile of worms. "You look as happy as a man who struck oil."

"I feel that happy, as crazy as that sounds." Kane grabbed the coffee can she'd brought with her that morning, then bent down and, using the lid, scooped the worms into the container. "Let's go fishing. For real this time."

Susannah watched him grab their poles, the same shiny new tackle box from the night before, and they marched on down the wooded path to the lake, Kane gleeful. She trailed along, not nearly as excited as Kane by the prospect of sitting on the dock and casting a hook into the water. She zipped her sweatshirt up, against the morning chill in the air, but Kane seemed oblivious to the low spring temperature. "You're really into this."

"Never done it before. I've heard it's fun. Relaxing."

"You've never fished?"

"I told you, I work a lot. Downtime isn't even in my vocabulary." He let out a deep breath, just as his cell phone started up again, for the fourth time that morning. Susannah had never known anyone whose cell phone rang as often as his did—and who answered as infrequently as Kane did. This time, Kane let out a curse, withdrew the cell from his jacket pocket, glanced at the number, shook his head, then tucked the phone away again. "What's first?"

"Bait your hook." She reached into the can, pulled out a worm and held up the slimy creature. "You've got to get this little guy on that tiny silver hook." She demonstrated, with a few quick nimble movements.

He arched a brow. "Not one ounce of squeamishness?

I'm impressed. I don't think any of the women I know would ever handle a worm, must less do what you just did."

"I grew up fishing. My dad loved coming here, and we used to fish together a lot." Her gaze drifted to the deep, green water, and she could swear her father's spirit still lingered here. His presence hung heavy in the budding maple trees, the rich earth, the soft whispers of the breeze. She closed her eyes and inhaled the sweet fresh air, and for a moment Susannah was ten again, spending a lazy summer afternoon with her father after his work was done for the day, learning more about life than about fishing.

Susannah opened her eyes and drank in the view again. She would miss this place. The memories that it held, the comfort she found here, like curling under a thick blanket on a cold winter's night. "Anyway," she finished, brushing off the memories before they worked their way into tears, "the main reason I'm not squeamish around this stuff is because I was the one hanging out at the lake after school. I'm not a girly-girl."

"Then you're perfect for me." He cleared his throat, as if he realized what he'd just said. "I meant for this week, of course."

"Of course."

He couldn't mean anything else, she decided. She didn't *want* him to. Did she?

No. She had plans, and those plans did not include being tied to anyone else, even a man with deep blue eyes and a teasing grin.

Kane wrestled with the wriggly worm, but after a couple of tries had it on his hook. Susannah rose and cast her line into the water, explaining her actions as she did it. "Now you try."

He leaned back, flipped the rod forward, but the hook fell short.

"Like this," Susannah said, slipping in behind him, intending only to show him, as she had been shown a thousand times before. She placed her right hand on his, her left arm on his waist. He glanced over his shoulder, bringing their cheeks together, and then, as natural as two blades of grass touching in the breeze, their lips. Had she kissed him, or had he kissed her?

She stopped keeping track because the feel of Kane's mouth against hers was agonizingly wonderful. Even as Susannah broke away and tried to get back to business, tried to ignore the dark desire lingering in Kane's gaze and his smile, a roaring zing of awareness ran through her. She knew this wasn't going to be an ordinary lesson in casting a hook into the water—because she was hooking herself, too.

If she was smart, she'd step away. Go back to show and tell. None of this hands-on instruction. Except every time her brain told her to do that, her hormones reminded her of that first kiss. And the second. And the third. Of the way Kane looked without a shirt. And then back to those kisses again. "Um, to cast a hook, you put your arm back like this," she said.

"Like this?" he repeated, his voice quiet, dark.

"Yeah." She leaned with him, his arm brushing against her chest, setting off a charge of explosions under her skin as if the fabric of her shirt and bra didn't exist. "And then you, uh, go forward, really fast, and uh, when you do, you let go of the button."

"Like this?" Kane asked again, in that same dark, deep voice, doing what she'd instructed, leaving Susannah's body behind with the movement. A whisper of disappointment whistled through her.

"Exactly." She stepped away, working a smile to her face when Kane's bobber popped up just a few feet away from her own. "You did it."

"Thanks to you. Now what do we do?"

"We wait."

He shot her a grin. "Any ideas on how to kill time?"

Oh, she had a hundred of them. None of them the usual ways she had killed time while fishing. Which had been talking, listening to music, sometimes even reading a book. But today, with Kane Lennox beside her, she didn't care one whit about catching a fish. Or watching the water. Or anything but continuing what they had started the night before.

"Why Paris?"

Of everything Kane could have asked her, that question took Susannah most by surprise. "What?"

"I noticed every poster, every decoration you have is about Paris. From all that, I assumed that was the first stop on your trip around the world. Why that city out of all the ones in the world?"

She jiggled her line a little, reeling in some before answering. Rover began digging in the dirt at the edge of the lake, trying to unearth a partially buried stick. "My parents were supposed to go on a honeymoon to Paris when they first got married, but they never did. My father's dad had a stroke just before the wedding, and my mom and dad ended up staying home to work his farmland out on County Road 9, just outside of town. Farmers work long days and never get vacations. My parents would take day trips here and there, but they never got to go on that big European trip they'd dreamed of."

"I know people like that," Kane said. "My uncle worked until the day he died. Had a heart attack in his office. Never even made it out of his chair. That's when I decided I better take a vacation and have the life I'd always wanted, even if it's only for a few days, before I ended up like him."

A smile crossed her face. "Seems we have something else in common. I never wanted a business that would consume my life like that farm did my parents'. I wanted a chance to see the world, except doing that's pretty expensive." She grinned. "Good thing I have this lucrative side job in fishing lessons."

He smiled back. "Good thing. You should consider tutoring all the clueless out-of-towners."

"Yeah, we get *tons* of those in Chapel Ridge."

He moved his rod a little to the side, pulling in the slack. "You're starting your travels with a great city."

The images of the Eiffel Tower, the banks of the Seine, the quaint bistros, all those places in Paris she'd imagined visiting and never touched, marched through Susannah's mind. "Have you been there?"

"Not as a tourist. Only on business."

"You must be pretty high up at the jewelry store to get to go to Paris."

Kane shrugged, and again Susannah could swear she detected that icy tension in his shoulders. "I suppose so."

"I'm planning on working my way through the rest of the world, one doggie shampoo at a time."

Kane reached out and clasped her hand in his own. "Paris in springtime will be a perfect way to start."

Thirty yards away, the red-and-white ball on the end of Kane's line dipped beneath the water, then popped back up again. "Hey! You've got a bite."

He began to turn the reel, but Susannah laid a hand on his. "Not yet. Give the pole a little jerk, then wait."

He did as she said. The bobber went under the water and didn't come back up.

"Feel anything?"

Kane went still. "Line's pulling."

"Now reel it in."

In slow and steady circles, Kane rolled the clear fishing line back onto the reel, inching the fish out of the water and back to the dock. A few minutes later, a six-inch bluegill dangled on the end of his line, flopping its yellow, green and blue body back and forth. "Will you look at that? I caught one. Already."

"He's big enough to eat. If you want to have him for dinner."

"No, I just want to catch them. I'm taking no prisoners." He grinned. "That's where the fun is, isn't it?" He finished pulling the fish in, then followed Susannah's instructions for removing the bluegill from the hook and releasing it gently back into the lake. The fish remained still against Kane's palm for a second, then swam off and disappeared beneath the dark surface. "Go ahead, go free," Kane said quietly. Then he cleared his throat, straightened and turned back to Susannah. "Let's do that again."

She laughed. "I can't believe you're paying me to teach you this."

"And I can't believe you're such a great instructor, with some amazing fringe benefits." He placed a quick kiss on her lips, then grabbed his pole and headed over to the bait bucket.

Fringe benefits? He'd made her sound like an insurance package or an extra vacation day. Disappointment sank like a stone in Susannah's gut, but she brushed it away. She didn't want any more than these few days.

Did she?

For the next half hour, they fished, with Kane reeling in another four fish, and Susannah catching three, throwing all of them back. After each catch, Kane was as happy as a miner discovering a vein of gold. "Had enough?"

He held up his fishing pole. "I'm ready for some marlin now."

She laughed. "You won't find those out here, but I'm glad you enjoyed the experience."

"I did." He took her hand and gave it a squeeze. "More than you know."

He leaned in to kiss her again when his phone began to ring, the sound cutting through the quiet of the lake and destroying the moment. He'd opened up more than just an old coffee can filled with worms today. All that time alone, waiting for the fish. Then the joy of finally catching one had Kane dropping his guard and opening a part of his heart to Susannah. He'd begun to feel something for her, something deeper than he'd felt for anyone before. He could practically hear the warning bells clanging. Where could he possibly take this from here? Chapel Ridge, Indiana, didn't go with Lennox Gem Corporation in New York City. And a woman like Susannah Wilson was never going to understand why a billionaire CEO had deceived her.

"I'll let you get that," Susannah said as the phone rang again. "I have to get to work so I can walk the shelter dogs. I'll catch up with you later. Okay?"

Susannah rose on her tiptoes and placed a kiss on Kane's cheek. The kiss was sweet, innocent and completely devoid of anything passionate, yet it touched a spot in Kane that he had thought New York and the business, and the world of money he inhabited, had burned away. As he watched her leave, her lithe figure moving easily up the hill and back to her car, he heard Rover let out a whine of disappointment. "I hear you, buddy. I feel the same way."

The phone continued its musical assault on his senses.

Kane fished the cursed electronic device out of his back pocket. Took one look at the silver ball and chain, then a second at Susannah and the fishing pole slung over her shoulder, and decided he couldn't do this right, not unless he did it all the way.

He turned back to face the lake, then flung the phone as far as he could. It landed with a satisfying plop, floated for a second, then sank to the bottom of Lake Everett, taking its still-ringing expectations deep into the silt.

"Suzie-Q, I need you."

"Jackie, I'm running out the door. I can't—"

"This isn't a favor. This is about Paul."

Susannah stopped in her tracks, her hand halfway to the doorknob. She knew that tone in Jackie's voice, knew it like the back of her hand. Jackie was having a crisis. Again. "What's wrong?"

"Paul called off the wedding."

"What? Why?"

A sob, a catch on the other end, then Jackie sniffled and continued. "He said…he's not ready. He thinks we're rushing. That we don't have enough money and we should wait until we've saved enough to buy a bigger house and have kids. But, Suzie, I don't want to wait. I love him."

Jackie and Paul had had this argument a hundred times over the past year. From the second Paul had slipped the ring onto Jackie's finger, he'd worried about finances. He'd calculated their budget from here to Sunday, trying to make two lean paychecks stretch further. Jackie, never one to worry about price tags or bill due dates, had argued with him more than once about the cost of the wedding.

Susannah could have saved him the breath. She'd been

trying to tell Jackie the same thing for years. But Jackie had never wanted to listen to talk about budgets and bills.

"It's just cold feet, Jackie. It'll be fine." She closed the books for The Sudsy Dog, gathered up that day's checks and the deposit slip, tucking both into her purse. Tess gave her a sympathetic smile as Susannah sent her a wave and headed out the door, mouthing a thank-you.

"I think it's more than that. Can you come over? Talk to me? I really don't want to be alone and you're so good at talking to me and making me feel better. Please, Suzie? I'm so worried."

"Aren't you at work?"

"Are you kidding me? I couldn't go back to work after Paul said that. I called in sick."

Susannah ran a hand over her face and bit back a scream of frustration. No matter how many times Susannah had tried to tell her differently, Jackie had never seemed to get the message about responsibility versus whim. "Jackie, you can't do that. You two need the money. Isn't that what this is really all about?"

"Well…yeah." She sniffled again. "But—"

"But what better way to send a message to Paul that you're on the same page as him than to keep earning your own paycheck?" Susannah paused, but got silence on the other end. She doubted Jackie was even listening. A hundred times Susannah had tried to instill a sense of responsibility, an understanding of priorities in Jackie, and gotten nowhere. Eventually it just became easier to do it all. "You should go back to work. Talk to me when you get home."

"Suzie, this is a *crisis*. How can I work when my life is *imploding?*"

She'd said the same thing last week when her dress fitting had made her feel fat. And two weeks before that when one of her bridesmaids had endured a breakup of her own. Jackie had been blessed with a patient boss, but even Susannah knew that patience could only be stretched so thin. Still, she kept all this to herself. No sense making Jackie any more upset. "Jackie, you're a receptionist at a paper company. It's not like you're in a high-stress, demanding job. Heck, after three the phone hardly ever rings over there. I'm sure you can get through the day."

"You have no sympathy at all. I can't believe you won't come home and take care of me. I need you to make me some soup and—"

Susannah leaned against her car and closed her eyes. She rubbed her temples and prayed for strength. "Jackie, I have other things to do."

"Yeah, okay." Jackie sighed. "I wish Mom was here. Don't you, Susannah? She'd make it better. She always knew what to do and say."

Guilt rocketed through Susannah. She refused to give in to the emotion. Refused to let it bother her. Refused to let it sing its siren song again.

And stop her from living her life one more time.

Kane had thought he'd have more time before they called out the bloodhounds.

He flung the newspaper into the wastebasket, but it was too late. The small headline, buried in the entertainment section of the paper—thank God for small favors—had already been burned into his memory. Gem Business CEO Missing: Family Spokesperson Says, "We're Worried."

Family spokesperson. Kane snorted. Another euphemism for Ronald Jeffries, his father's lawyer. The man called on to do all of Elliott Lennox's dirty work. Like deal with a wayward son yet again. His father had to be royally ticked off to have alerted the media.

Kane reached for his cell phone, then remembered. It had found a permanent home at the bottom of the lake. There'd be no calling home. Just as well. He wanted an escape. If he picked up a phone and called his father, there'd be a limo here in five minutes.

To drag Kane back to the life he so desperately wanted to leave, just for a little while.

He turned to enter the hardware store, when he saw Susannah coming out of her shop a few doors down. She had her keys out, her thumb on the remote for her car, when she saw him.

"Kane," she began, heading down the sidewalk to him, her steps fast, her face devoid of its earlier smile. "I can't meet with you this afternoon." She dug in her purse, then pulled out the bills he'd handed her earlier. "Let me refund your money."

He waved off the cash. "Keep it. We'll catch up later. What's wrong?"

"It's Jackie. She's in a 'crisis.'"

"I take it the world isn't coming to an end?"

Susannah laughed, and he could hear the relief explode in the sound, as if she were a bomb of stress waiting for just the right detonator. "No. Just Paul, worrying about the bills. They argued again. Called off the wedding. Again."

"This has happened before?" Then he remembered Paul's words in the bar about Jackie's spending. Clearly the issue was a source of friction between practical Paul and flighty Jackie.

"Jackie isn't what anyone would call responsible with money. And Paul probably found out that she spent too much on flowers or a veil or something silly like little plastic people to sit at the base of the cake and look like extras."

"Extras?"

Susannah nodded. "Jackie wanted to include representatives of every guest on the cake."

"Sounds to me like it'll look more like an ant farm gone horribly awry."

Laughter burst out of Susannah in a steady stream. She laughed so hard, her cheeks turned red, and her eyes began to water. "Oh, Lord, I needed that today. Thanks, Kane." She laid a hand on him, an innocent touch, the kind meant only to express gratitude, but it sent a rocket of desire roaring through Kane's body.

Susannah turned to go, and Kane knew he should let her leave. Let her deal with her family on her own. He had no need for entanglements. No wish to get involved. He was going back at the end of this week, back to a life that was as far removed from this town as Mars was from the moon.

He needed to get real here—and fast. This relationship with Susannah would never work in his world, no matter how much he might think otherwise while he was inhabiting this little slice of heaven. Except…a part of him kept on hoping the Utopia would just go right on existing.

"Susannah, wait."

She pivoted back. "Yeah?"

"Need some help? Money is one thing I'm pretty good at."

And when a smile curved across her face, Kane realized he had a problem. One all the money in the world couldn't fix.

He wanted to move the moon right next to Mars.

Jackie hyperventilated with the best of them.

Susannah sat in the kitchen with her sister, doling out

coffee and cookies, waiting for the emotional storm to pass. It turned out Paul hadn't actually called off the wedding— Jackie also had a tendency toward hyperbole—but the two of them had had yet another finances disagreement, which Jackie took as a sign of impending doom. Now, Kane leaned against the opposite corner, Rover at his feet, the two males reflecting twin pained expressions.

"What am I going to do? Paul is never going to listen to me after we get married. He's always all money this, and money that." A pile of shredded tissues lay before Jackie, beside a plate of cookie crumbs.

"Be more responsible, for one," Susannah said. "You spend money like it's pouring out of the faucet and—"

Jackie let out a gust. "I don't want to hear one more word about responsibility and boring things like money, Suzie. That's not fun. For Pete's sake, I'm getting married, not *dying*."

Kane pushed off from the countertop. "If you don't start worrying about money, you *will* die."

Susannah opened her mouth, closed it, opened it again, then finally shut it. And waited to see what Kane had to say next.

Beside her, Jackie stared at him, as if he'd just pronounced the sky brown.

Kane crossed to the table, pulled out a chair and took a seat, not swinging it around and sitting backwards like Paul did, but instead lowering himself as properly as a guest at a dinner party. "I don't mean die literally, but it'll be close to the same thing." He leaned forward, capturing Jackie's attention in that direct way he had of holding eye contact. Even Susannah found herself wrapped around his every word. "You need money to have a marriage. To have a life. Not millions of dollars, of course, but enough to pay your bills, to fund your future. Your retirement."

Jackie waved off the words. "Retirement is, like, ten million years away."

"Maybe not quite that far, but yes, you do have quite a few years. All the more reason to start saving now. Did you know that if you and Paul started putting aside just a couple hundred dollars a month, you'd retire as millionaires?"

Jackie's eyes widened. "*Millionaires?* Us? But…he's a teacher. I'm a receptionist. We can't be millionaires."

"Everyone can be a millionaire, Jackie, with the right investment strategy. You just have to be smart about your money."

"Smart? Yeah, right." She snorted, then chewed on her lip and considered that for a moment. "We'd really be millionaires?"

"Yes."

"Like, what would I have to do?" she asked, grabbing her wedding planner from the center of the table. She flipped to a blank page, poised a pen over the lined pink paper and waited for Kane's answer.

Susannah gaped at Kane, as he began to rattle off easy, step-by-step advice about 401k plans and IRAs, while Jackie scribbled. He had done what Susannah had never been able to do, in all the years she'd been talking to Jackie, thousands of words falling on deaf ears. He'd gotten her attention, and gotten Jackie to actually ask questions, take his advice, and commit it to paper. Whether she'd actually do it would be another story, but Susannah had a feeling, based on Jackie's rapt expression, that things were about to change.

At least financially.

A few minutes later, Jackie clutched the book to her chest and got up from the table. "I'm going to go call Paul, and tell him I have a…" She glanced at Kane. "What did you call it?"

"Roadmap for your financial future."

"A roadmap for our financial future." She beamed. "Maybe if he hears that, he'll see that I'm serious about money, and he won't be so worried about the wedding."

"I know Paul, and I know he'll feel better if you're both on the same page with budgets and finances," Kane said. "I think it will all work out splendidly, as long as you stick to that plan."

Jackie leaned down and gave Kane a tight, quick hug, and a kiss on the cheek. "Thank you. You really are the best man." Then she bounded off to her room, so fast, she didn't see the look of surprise on Kane's face.

"You're a miracle worker," Susannah said.

"It was nothing."

"Are you kidding me? I've been lecturing my sister about money for eight years, and yet she still spent and spent like she had an unlimited supply. It's been a constant source of friction between me and her, and her and Paul. And yet, here you come along, and in five minutes you've transformed her."

He laughed. "All I did was get her attention. Doesn't mean it'll stick, but I think once she gets married, and she and Paul have some serious discussions, things will turn around."

"If they could even turn thirty degrees, I'd be happy." Susannah rose, depositing the dishes into the sink. She ran the water over them, washed the few cups and plates, and loaded them into the strainer.

She sensed Kane behind her before she saw him. His presence, his cologne, the warmth of his body. She stilled, holding her breath, waiting for what would come next. So very aware of how alone they were now. Would he touch her? Would he kiss her? Or would he simply walk away?

He reached up and trailed a finger down her neck, a slow, easy touch that—oh, God—set every nerve ending on fire, igniting parts of Susannah's body that she didn't even know could come alive. She gripped the countertop and closed her eyes, then tipped her head to one side as Kane leaned forward, brushed the hair away from her neck and pressed his lips to the tender hollow of skin.

All thoughts of her sister, money and anything resembling reality disappeared. She forgot every reason she had for not getting involved with him. Couldn't have come up with a single sentence about why walking away from Kane before she got in any deeper would be a good idea. Because—oh, oh—he was here and he was there, and sensations were exploding in her head, along her skin.

Everywhere.

A mewl escaped her. Kane trailed the kisses down along her jaw, turning her as he did, brushing up against her lips, but not touching them. Not yet. Anticipation boiled inside her, and Susannah arched against him, her mouth open, waiting, wanting. Needing him.

His hands cupped her chin, and those eyes—those penetrating blue eyes—captured hers for a long, quiet moment. Then he leaned forward, and kissed her, slowly, sweetly, as if savoring every inch of her.

He kissed her like a composer writing a symphony. Every nerve ending sang, every touch created a concert. Susannah's arms reached around his back, held him close, as close as she could, and yet, still, it wasn't enough. Not nearly enough.

Kane drew back, an easy smile on his lips. "What do you say we get back to what we were doing earlier?"

"I thought we just did."

He chuckled. "If I remember right, I bought and paid for your services. And now that the crisis is averted, you're all mine again."

Those four words sent a tempting thrill through Susannah. "And what would you like me to teach you now?"

He closed the gap between them, his lips a breath away from hers. "To start a fire."

Then he kissed her again. And started one of his own.

CHAPTER NINE

STONES spit in a wave behind the tires of the rental car as Kane skidded to a stop in front of the cabin. Damn. He saw the guest standing on his porch and the item in her hands, both shadowed by the wooden overhang, and his instincts told him one thing.

The vacation was over.

"Wait here a second, will you?" Kane said.

"Sure." But Susannah's face showed her confusion at being left behind.

What could he say? *Sorry to tell you one thing about who I was, but the truth is about to come out? Everything I've said has been a lie, but hold on a second before you hate me, I had really great reasons for keeping my identity a secret?*

Instead he didn't say anything at all.

The dread in Kane's stomach grew as he got out of the car, Rover scrambling behind him before he could leave the dog in the car. Kane crossed to the porch of the cabin and greeted Mrs. Maxwell. He watched her face, to see if she recognized him as *the* Kane Lennox. Had she read the paper? Had she put the pieces together?

Had she, most of all, called his father? Or had his father finally found him?

"Mrs. Maxwell. Nice to see you again."

The gray-haired woman bent down and greeted the spaniel, who had yet to meet a person he didn't slobber over with a friendly greeting. Rover swished against her, his tail beating a hello into Mrs. Maxwell's floral-print housedress. "I see you made a friend with your stray. Did you give him a name?"

"I'm not keeping him. I'd hoped you might have heard about a missing dog."

"Not yet. Or at least, no one has said a word to me. I checked the *Chapel Ridge Post*, too, and there hasn't been a single lost dog ad in there all week. Pity, too. He's such a cute little booger. Someone must be heartbroken."

"Yes, I'm sure they are." So heartbroken they hadn't even noticed the dog had disappeared. "I'll hang a sign up downtown or something, then." Get to the point, he wanted to shout, but he didn't. Clearly, Mrs. Maxwell hadn't figured out who he was. To her, he was still another vacationer.

"Good idea." She straightened, her gray curls bouncing with the movement, then held out the envelope he'd seen earlier. Even from the car, Kane had recognized the distinctive white envelope and bright colors marking an overnight delivery. "This is for you. It came to the rental office, which is where all the mail for the cabins is delivered. I figured it must be important, which is why I drove it out here myself. What a lucky thing that you came home just after I got here. I was going to leave it by the door if you didn't come by, but—"

"Thank you, Mrs. Maxwell." Kane gave her a pointed look, and took the envelope.

"Oh, you're welcome." She remained standing on the porch, arms crossed. Then she looked at him, at the envelope and back at him. "Aren't you going to open it? It's probably pretty important, being one of those overnight things and all. I never get those. I can't even remember the last time a renter got one."

"I know what's in it," Kane said. "I've been expecting this." He'd known his father would find him eventually. Elliott Lennox got what he wanted. Every time.

And what he wanted—what he always wanted—was control over everyone in his life. Especially Kane.

The sharp edges of the envelope only added to Kane's resentment. When would his father see his son as a *son,* not a commodity? Notice him as a blood relative, instead of another stone in the Lennox family necklace?

Mrs. Maxwell pushed her glasses further up her nose. "Well, I suppose I better get back to the office. I have…" Her voice trailed off, then she cupped a hand over her eyes, shielding them from the sun. "Oh my. Is that *Susannah Wilson* in your car?"

He had never been in such a nosy town. In New York, people walked by and looked right through him. Sure, there was espionage and spying, but it was of the corporate kind. Not the personal kind. "Uh, yeah. She's…helping me with the dog."

"She's single, you know." Mrs. Maxwell gave him a knowing nod. "One of our most eligible bachelorettes."

"Thank you again for coming by, Mrs. Maxwell," Kane said, withdrawing a bill from his pocket and handing it to the woman.

"What's this? A tip? Oh, goodness. I don't expect a tip." She pushed the money back at him. "This isn't some big city. We don't take money for simple things like delivering someone's mail." Mrs. Maxwell shook her head and laughed. "This is Chapel Ridge, Mr. Lennox. People here do things just because."

Then she headed down his porch toward her car, sending Susannah a friendly wave and a hello as she did.

Kane marveled at Mrs. Maxwell's comment. *Just because.*

How unlike his world. He'd been wrong. This wasn't nosiness. It was more…concern. Interest. The beginnings of relationships.

What Kane had found in Chapel Ridge hadn't been simply a vacation from his job, a host of new experiences, but also a community of people who embraced each other, supported each other and welcomed strangers as if they were their own family.

Susannah got out of the car, carrying the takeout they'd picked up at the Corner Kitchen on the way over, and met him on the stoop. "All set?"

"Yes. Thank you for waiting. Just a little…business to conduct."

"For your job?"

"Yes."

"The jewelry store you work for sent you an overnight package?" Susannah cast a dubious glance at the envelope. "You must be pretty important to them if they're bothering you on vacation."

She gave him a suspicious look. Damn. Once again he had said too much, let too many details out. Twisted his cover story a little too many times. "How about an early dinner? I'm starving. And if we can get a fire started, we can break this chill."

"Sure. Do you have kindling? Matches?"

"Check and check."

"Then let me show you how to make fire. By the end of the day, you'll feel like a real caveman." Susannah grinned, then brushed past him and into the cabin.

Kane glanced down at the envelope, noting the return

address in New York. No matter what happened today, he'd already been reminded that he was still more of a prisoner of his life than ever.

A shadow had dropped over Kane's face, and had yet to disappear. Susannah watched the flames flicker across his features, and knew that envelope he'd received earlier had something to do with the change.

But what? And why?

She'd heard him tell Mrs. Maxwell he'd been expecting the delivery. Was the arrival of some work during a vacation such an annoyance? Or could the package contain bad news? Even in the close quarters of the cabin, Kane had managed to put distance between them, as if he didn't want to talk about whatever sat heavy on his mind. Susannah had thought she and Kane had drawn closer over the last few days. Close enough, at least, for him to tell her about something monumental.

Apparently, she'd been wrong.

"Are you ready for tonight?" he asked, disrupting her thoughts.

"Tonight?"

"The rehearsal. Paul is as nervous as a cat about to take a bath." Kane chuckled, lightening the tension in his face and shoulders. He slipped into his old self, or at least a closer facsimile. "When I spoke to him about it, he was as antsy as he used to be back in college before a big exam."

"Paul got antsy? He's one of the calmest guys I know— unless of course he's talking to Jackie about money."

Kane rose, hung the fireplace poker back on the rack and crossed to the small efficiency kitchen. He began unpacking the takeout bags from the Corner Kitchen, loading the packages onto the tiny wooden kitchen table. "You didn't know Paul in college. He was a little… wilder."

"And you?" Susannah asked, approaching Kane. "What were you like in college?"

"Most of the time, I was…subdued and sedate. Well mannered."

She scoffed. "Right. Show me a guy who acts like that in college. Especially when there are pretty coeds and beer around? Paul told me a few stories about his years at Northwestern. The edited versions, I'm sure, but I got the impression he went to more than a few parties." Susannah retrieved some paper plates and plastic silverware from inside one of the cabinets and brought them back to the table, then pulled up one of the two chairs and took a seat.

Kane settled into the opposite chair, and the two of them began passing the Corner Kitchen dishes back and forth, heaping mashed potatoes, homemade meat loaf, gravy and green beans baked with bacon bits onto their plates. "Paul has stories. Me, not so many."

She cocked her head and studied him. "You roomed next door to Paul. Hung out together. How could that be?"

"I…" Kane pulled a biscuit out of the paper bag, followed by a butter packet, then hesitated before opening it. "I had a chaperone, of sorts."

"You? Were you some kind of troublemaker or something?"

He scoffed. "Not at all. My father just felt like I needed a keeper."

"A keeper?" Susannah blinked. Parents still did that kind of thing in the twentieth century? It seemed impossible to believe, yet, it explained a lot about Kane. His inexperience at the simplest of life events. What kind of childhood had the man had? And why? "I can't imagine having such a strict upbringing."

"There were a lot of expectations on my shoulders." He toyed with the edge of the envelope, still unopened. "There still are, to be honest."

"Are some of them in there?"

He jerked to attention, as if he'd just realized he'd said too much. Then his gaze broke from hers and tension poured like steel into his frame.

What was with Kane? And for that matter, what was he hiding? Every time she tried to get close, tried to ask more than a few questions, he clammed up and changed the subject.

She was tired of this "Just Kane," "Just Susannah" game. She wanted more—a real connection. Even if it was only for a few days, she wanted something more satisfying than a taste of whipped cream. She wanted the whole cake.

She knew so little about him. A snippet here. A snippet there. As if he was showing her the photo album of his life, but with all the identifying details removed from the images. Why?

Didn't he trust her? Or was he that intent on leaving at the end of his trip—and leaving all ties to Chapel Ridge behind?

"This food is great," Kane said. "Have you tried the meat loaf? Do you think the owners will sell me the recipe?"

Now they were talking *meat loaf?* She wanted to know *him,* not his preferences in the baked ground beef department. Suddenly, the past days rose to the surface, the frustration threatening to explode.

"Did you grow up in a bubble or something? Honestly, who has never had meat loaf? It was like a staple in my house, and virtually everyone else's I knew, too. Every Friday night, like it or not. When I grew up and started making my own dinners, I refused to cook it because I was so tired of eating meat loaf. Now I crave it every once in a while, oddly enough."

Kane shook his head. "My mother wasn't the meat loaf kind."

"Whoa, there's a whole lot of information."

"What's that supposed to mean?"

"It means I know almost nothing about you," she said. "I feel like I'm dealing with a crossword puzzle every time I try to have a conversation with you, Kane. I know you've never walked barefoot on grass. Had a keeper in college. Had a dad who ruled your life, and wow, here's a clue, your mom didn't make meat loaf. What the heck am I supposed to figure from that?" She rose and spun away from the table, placing her plate on the countertop. "You know almost everything about me and I…" She looked down at the dog sleeping at his feet. "I know more about this stray than I do you."

Kane shifted in his chair. Outside, birds called to each other, the breeze sent a branch scraping against the cabin window. Rover raised his head, then went back to sleep. Kane took in a breath, let it out. "You're right. I have been rather guarded about my life. And I owe you an apology for that." He ran a hand through his hair, displacing the dark waves. "If I tell you something, will you keep it between us?"

She sensed an opening in the wall, a chink about to be removed. "Of course."

"My family had a lot of money when I was growing up. So I'm not used to—" he waved around the room "—this. Any of this, especially not meat loaf. Or cheese that comes in packages, or fishing with live worms." He smiled. "I got a taste of real life, of what could be something close to it, in college when I met Paul and had brief moments of freedom. That's why I'm here. I'm far too old to keep going through life never really experiencing it. When Paul asked me to be his best man, I seized the opportunity to see the world from the other side of the fence. *Carpe diem*, and all that."

"Then, after the wedding, you plan on going back to New York, to your regular world."

"Right."

"No strings, no attachments."

His gaze met hers. Direct. Honest. "Exactly."

Whatever part of Susannah might have hoped for otherwise—if there had been a part—knew now there would be nothing more than these kisses. The dance by the lake. And whatever came of the wedding tomorrow. She should be happy, because she was leaving town herself on Saturday and knew how foolish it would be to hold on to any romantic notices of being whisked away to some hide-away chapel at the end of this week, but nevertheless, a whisper of disappointment ran through her, then settled heavy in her gut.

He wanted nothing more than these few days.

He didn't want her. And that was exactly what she'd thought she wanted, too—

Until she got it.

"So," she said, working a smile to her face, telling herself this was perfect, that people who focused on romance and dreams left themselves open to being hurt, "what else did you want to experience while you're here?"

His smile met hers, and a long moment of quiet extended between them. "One more dance, Susannah, that's all."

The minister cleared his throat. Looked at his watch. Cleared his throat a second time. "Do you have any idea where they might be?"

"No." Susannah glanced toward the front of Chapel Ridge Lutheran Church, but no one came through the doors. Jackie's bridesmaids sat in the front pews, Paul's groomsmen beside them. Up in the balcony, Mrs. Maxwell watched it all from her perch at the organ, probably taking notes for the town gossips. "Maybe they forgot?"

"Their own wedding rehearsal?" Pastor Weatherly said.

"I'll try Jackie's cell phone again." Susannah pulled her Nokia out of her purse and punched in her sister's number. Three rings and then finally, Jackie picked up with a breathless hello. "*Jackie!* Where are you?"

She giggled. "Umm…making up with Paul."

"Well, stop," Susannah whispered, heading down the aisle and out of earshot of everyone else. "You're supposed to be at the wedding rehearsal."

"Oh! I totally forgot." She giggled some more. "Uh, oh, Paul, stop, stop, honey. Oh, oooh, um, Suzie, could you please, uh, oh, Paul—"

Susannah cringed. There were just certain things she didn't want to know or hear about her sister's life. "Jackie! I absolutely refuse to listen to you and Paul have…fun. So will you quit that for five minutes and talk to me?"

"Okay, okay. I'm here. Actually, I'm in Indianapolis. So it'll be like, twenty or thirty minutes before I'm back in Chapel Ridge. Maybe, uh, more." She giggled some more.

"Indianapolis!" Susannah cast her gaze to the stained-glass images on the windows, begging for patience from the jewel-toned disciples. "What are you doing there?"

"Paul and I went down to pick up the tuxes. This is where that shop was that had the special ones I really liked, remember? And after we got them, we stopped for dinner, and then we got to talking, and then, well, we got…side-tracked. So we pulled over."

"Jackie, this is important. Don't you care? This is *your* wedding, not mine."

"Suzie, you'll take care of it for me, won't you? I'll be there soon."

Susannah ran a hand through her hair and sighed. "I don't have a choice, do I?" She hung up the phone, strode back to the front of the church and pasted a bright smile on her face. "Jackie's on her way. She'll be a little while, though. She got…tied up when they went to get the tuxes."

Pastor Weatherly flicked out his wrist. "I can't wait that long, Susannah, I'm sorry. I have a funeral here in an hour and I know you all have reservations for the rehearsal dinner, too."

"Can we reschedule? We still need to run through the wedding, at least so everyone knows where to stand. And without Paul and Jackie…"

The minister thought for a second. "I have a baptism in the morning, then another wedding before Jackie's. I just don't see another time to do this. Do we have other people who could substitute for them tonight? Then perhaps you could explain the steps to Jackie and Paul tomorrow? And if she gets here early enough tonight, I should have time for another quick run through." Pastor Weatherly looked at the women and men sitting in the pews, chatting quietly among themselves. "For tonight, all I need is a man and a woman."

Paul's single friends skulked down in the pews with that don't-look-at-me expression. Before the minister could choose a volunteer, Kane stepped over to Susannah and took her hand. "That would be us, wouldn't it?"

"Us? Are you kidding me?"

"Isn't that the job of the best man and the maid of honor? To step in as needed?"

"Uh…well…I don't think he meant literally."

But Kane was already leading her up the aisle and to the edge of the altar. "We'll do it, Pastor."

"Wonderful." He beamed at them, as if they were the bridal couple. "And your name is?"

"Kane. Kane Lennox."

"Ah, like in the Bible? The proverbial first son, who also, might I add, committed the very first murder." Pastor Weatherly gave Kane a good-natured smile. "Not that you, of course, are a felon in the making."

"Not at all, sir. And my name is spelled entirely different. Plus," he leaned forward, "I'm an only child, so there's no worry about fratricide."

Pastor Weatherly laughed. "Glad to hear it, son. Okay, Kane, you take your place to my left. And, Susannah, you can go back a few pews and make the march."

Susannah blanched. Walk down the aisle? Join Kane at the altar? This was crazy. "I really don't think that's necessary."

"Someone has to do it, and if we can at least complete this run-through, it will make everything so much easier tomorrow. Susannah, I know you'll be there to make sure everything goes smoothly for Jackie." Pastor Weatherly laid a hand on Susannah's arm. "Thank the Lord that she has had you all these years to watch out for her. You've been a wonderful sister."

"I know your time is limited, Pastor. We should get started," Susannah said, suddenly feeling hot, confined. She wanted to run from the church, from the praise the minister was heaping on her. If she'd done such a good job finishing the raising of her sister, wouldn't Jackie be here right now? Being responsible instead of being selfish?

Susannah headed to the back of the church. The other bridesmaids slipped into place before her, while the groomsmen took their places on the altar. Pastor Weatherly cued Mrs. Maxwell to begin playing the bridal march, from her perch at the organ up in the balcony. When the music began, Susannah took her first steps, clutching an imaginary bouquet. At first, she walked fast, hoping to get in, get out and make this go as fast as possible.

But then she caught Kane watching her, his cobalt eyes direct on hers, with that piercing way he had, and her steps faltered, then slowed. Her heart began to race, and her breath caught in her throat. The rest of the church dropped away, the other people blending into the background. All she saw was Kane, and the bemused smile on his face waiting for her to join him at the end of the aisle.

What if this were real? What if she were marrying him tonight? How would that feel?

Terrifying?

Or wonderful?

To see him every day from here on? To wake up to those cobalt eyes? To feel those arms around her until the day she died?

The wedding march came to a close as she made the final steps. Kane put out his hand and took hers, leading her up the two stairs to the altar. "You look beautiful when you smile like that," he whispered.

She opened her mouth to speak, but nothing came out, not so much as a breath. For the first time in her life, Susannah Wilson was totally, completely speechless.

"This is where I start the 'Dearly beloved, we are gathered…' part," Pastor Weatherly said. "And everybody tunes out for a few minutes as we go over a couple of Bible passages, sing one hymn that your sister picked out—"

"Jackie picked out a hymn for the ceremony?"

"Yes." Pastor Weatherly looked down at his notes. "'How Great Thou Art.'"

"Our mother's favorite," she whispered. And then she could hear the soft strains of her mother's voice, singing the song in church, or while she did the dishes, the stanzas carrying clear and strong, the notes lingering in the air long after she finished. How great…and, oh, how much Susannah missed those sweet vocals.

Her eyes filled with unshed tears, and the room blurred. The grief she held in check, always kept behind a firm wall, threatened to spill forward. "I…I had no idea she remembered."

Pastor Weatherly reached out a kind hand to Susannah and held hers for a long moment, his soft brown eyes telling her he understood everything. "She wanted to include Eleanor as much as she could."

Susannah smiled her gratitude to the minister, and the gesture wobbled a little on her face. For a moment, it felt as if her mother was right there, watching from the pews. Tomorrow, in the song, Susannah knew she would hear her mother's voice. What a wonderful touch, and for Jackie to think of it meant her sister was more aware of the important elements of the wedding than Susannah had thought. Her heart clenched, and she swiped at her eyes with the back of her hands. "We, um, should get started, Pastor Weatherly," she said, to change the subject, before she started crying. "You have your funeral tonight. Who died, by the way?"

"Jerry Linkheart. You probably don't remember him because he lived here before you were born, Susannah. He just moved back to town last week after he retired. Saddest thing, too." Pastor Weatherly shook his head. "It was only Jerry and his dog. Family said they haven't seen the dog in days. I guess little Bandit ran off when Jerry died. He had a heart attack at home."

"Would Bandit happen to be a Brittany spaniel?" Kane asked.

"He is indeed. Jerry loved that dog. Spoiled it rotten, from what I hear, though I suspect Bandit was just his little buddy. Either way, his sister told me she's glad it's gone. I get the feeling she's not much of a dog person. If you see it, Susannah, find the poor thing a good home, will you? That's what Jerry would want."

"I already did find the dog, or rather Kane here did. Out by his lake cottage."

The minister nodded. "Jerry lived down by the lake. Sounds like we've got Bandit. I'll call the family, see if it's okay with them if Kane keeps him. I don't think they want the dog."

Kane started shaking his head. "I, ah—"

"That would be great," Susannah cut in. Even if Kane didn't take Bandit, she would find a good home for the dog.

"Okay," Pastor Weatherly said, addressing first Kane and Susannah, then the few people in the pews, "we've got a happy ending for the dog. Let's get back to our happily-ever-after work here. We have a wedding to rehearse. After the hymn, we get to the good part. Kane, this is where you turn to Susannah."

"Uh, Jackie," Susannah corrected. No way did she want anyone thinking it was her and Kane getting married. It all felt way too realistic, standing up here, flanked by bridesmaids and groomsmen, instead of being one of the bridesmaids.

"Of course," Pastor Weatherly said. "Susannah, who is pretending to be Jackie, and Kane, who is pretending to be Paul." He grinned. "Wouldn't want me to marry the two of you tonight by accident, now, would you?"

"No," Kane and Susannah said at the same time.

Pastor Weatherly chuckled. "Well, let's pretend instead, 'Jackie' and 'Paul.' You two need to turn toward each other." He waved his hands together.

Susannah shifted her position at the same time Kane did. Acute awareness of him rocketed through her. Of where they were. Of the minister watching them. Of how easily this could, as Pastor Weatherly had said, be them getting married—

Instead of Jackie and Paul.

Would that be so bad?

Of course it would. She didn't want to get married. Didn't want to settle down. Not before she'd had her chance to explore the world, see something beyond the bounds of Chapel Ridge.

Except…she really liked Kane Lennox. His direct way of confronting problems—like the dog. Like Jackie.

Like her.

And there was something about him, something she'd glimpsed when he'd finally peeled back the layers and allowed her a peek into his world, that showed a man with vulnerabilities. Areas she wanted to know more about, even while she knew she should keep her focus on her ultimate goals, and on the fact that he was leaving and she was doing her best not to create any more ties in a life that already had too many….

She kept losing track of that resolve.

"First, I will ask each of you the same question," Pastor Weatherly said, interrupting her thoughts. "And you respond, 'I will.' Okay?"

Kane and Susannah nodded. But would she if this were real?

Before she could decide, Pastor Weatherly opened the leather-bound *Book of Common Prayer* in his hand, smoothed down the page and began to read. "Susannah, will you have this man to be your husband; to live together in the covenant of marriage? Will you love him, comfort him, honor and keep him, in sickness and in health; and, forsaking all others, be faithful to him as long as you both shall live?"

Susannah swallowed hard. Love him. Keep him. Be faithful. As long as she lived?

This was insane.

These were powerful words. *Permanent* words.

But it was all an act. Imaginary. Standing in for someone else. Not her life, not her marriage. "I will," she said, the words squeaking past her throat.

"Kane, will you have this woman to be—"

"He will," Susannah cut in. "You know Paul is going to say yes."

The minister smiled. "Of course he will. Okay, let's move on. Next, I address the congregation. Then we read a psalm, have a prayer, and read a couple of Bible passages. Then we move on to the part that gets you *really* hitched." Pastor Weatherly grinned, then turned back to Kane. "You two will have to run through these details with Paul and Jackie, but tell them not to worry if they forget. I'll be here to coach them. Kane, take Susannah's right hand in yours, then repeat after me, okay?"

Kane nodded. He reached up, took Susannah's hand in his, the touch sending a charge through her. One she couldn't ignore. Couldn't pretend was part of the act. Susannah shifted on her feet, but there was nowhere to go. Nowhere but right where she was.

"In the Name of God, I, Kane," Pastor Weatherly began to recite, "take you, Susannah, to be my wife…"

Kane's gaze met Susannah's. Butterflies raised a riot in

her gut, and she would have run from the church if he hadn't been holding her hand. "In the Name of God, I, Kane," he said, his voice soft, almost tender, "take you, Susannah, to be my wife…"

"To have and to hold from this day forward, for better, for worse, for richer, for poorer…"

Kane's hold on her hand tightened. Because he too wanted to run? Because he sensed her quivering? He ran a thumb over the back of her hand, and the butterflies roared, then began to quiet. "To have and to hold from this day forward, for better, for worse, for richer, for poorer…" On the last, a slight smile curved across his face.

"In sickness and in health, to love and to cherish, until we are parted by death. This is my solemn vow."

Kane reached up with his other hand and captured her free one. His cobalt eyes never left hers. The world closed in, leaving just the two of them on the altar. "In sickness and in health, to love and to cherish," he said, the words quietly, deliberately, "until we are parted by death. This is my solemn vow."

The last sentences seemed to hang in the air. Susannah gulped. This was supposed to be a joke, the two of them just filling in. But somewhere along the way, something had shifted, and a sense of reality had invaded the space between them.

A hush fell over the church, as if every single person was holding their collective breaths. Susannah's heart got caught in Kane's smile, in the words he'd just said.

How long had she waited to hear those very same words? For her turn at the life she'd seen everyone else have? The life she had set aside the day her parents died, so she could raise Jackie and give that gift of freedom instead to her sister?

And here in the church, for just a second, Susannah had become caught in the web of the fairy tale. She'd heard a gorgeous man pledge undying love. Even if he was only acting, Susannah closed her eyes, holding on to the fantasy for one moment longer.

Kane promising to love her. Forever.

"Now, Susannah," Pastor Weatherly said, "it's your turn. Keep holding Kane's hand and repeat after me. In the Name of God, I, Susannah, take you, Kane, to be my husband…"

Kane.

A husband. *Her* husband.

Susannah opened her mouth to speak, but the words refused to come. A rush of fear flooded her senses, and suddenly she couldn't breathe.

"Susannah," Pastor Weatherly whispered, "you're supposed to repeat what I said."

Kane's smile curved wider. "Changed your mind about having and holding me?"

"I…I can't do this," she said, spinning out of Kane's grasp. "I'm sorry."

Then she hurried out of the church and didn't stop running until she reached wide-open grass and fresh air.

The scent of freedom, the one thing she had craved for years. And refused to chance losing. Not even on an imaginary basis.

CHAPTER TEN

WHAT the hell was *that?*

Had he just gotten *married?*

Whether for real or not, for a few minutes there, Kane had been swept up into the moment and had, indeed, felt like he and Susannah were pledging to be together forever. And the crazy part?

He hadn't minded a bit.

Standing on that altar, she had looked beautiful, almost angelic. The setting sun streaming through the stained-glass windows had cast tiny rainbows across her features, like miniature jewels in her hair, on her skin.

And suddenly, his world, which had seemed so hard and cold a week ago, filled with sunshine. He couldn't imagine returning to New York, returning to work, to his penthouse apartment overlooking Central Park—

Without that.

Without her.

"Maybe that wasn't such a good idea," Pastor Weatherly said, as the rest of the wedding party began to file out of the church and head to their cars, their chattering voices expressing their surprise about what had happened. One of the groomsmen called over his shoulder to Kane that they were planning on meeting at the Corner Kitchen for the re-hearsal dinner. Kane nodded agreement.

"It did seem to backfire," Kane said.

"Perhaps Susannah didn't like being in the spotlight," Pastor Weatherly said, taking a seat on the top step of the altar. He gestured to Kane to join him.

Kane suspected more was involved in Susannah's reaction. If she'd even experienced a tenth of what he had up there on that altar, of that eerie sense of reality surround-ing them, as if he had on a tux and she a dress and veil in-stead of Jackie and Paul—then Kane couldn't blame her for running. "Maybe. Either way Jackie shouldn't have put Susannah in that situation in the first place."

"Well, that's kind of Jackie's way. She's a little…for-getful. And Susannah, well, she'd do about anything for Jackie, and she always has, ever since their parents died when Susannah was eighteen."

"Their parents are *both* dead?" Kane hadn't put those pieces together. Both her parents were gone, and at such a young age. He'd lost his own mother to cancer in college, and noticed his father had drawn even further into himself and the business. But to lose both parents—

That explained so much. Her commitment to her sister. Her emphasis on responsibility. And most of all her desire to leave, and finally live her own life.

The minister nodded. "I baptized those girls, and buried their parents eight years ago." He glanced over at Kane and read the clear question in the other man's eyes. "A boating accident. The Wilsons were fishing out on Lake Michigan when this storm came, out of nowhere. Their boat swamped when they were trying to get back to shore and they drowned."

Kane's gaze went to the doors. "Susannah was so young."

"Old enough to have her own life, but she chose instead to put that on hold and raise Jackie. Let me tell you, that girl was a handful at fourteen, bless her heart. But Susannah wouldn't have any part of breaking up her family. Jackie had lived in that house all her life, and Susannah refused to move her from there, or from the town that loved her." Pastor Weatherly laid a hand on Kane's. "After tomorrow, it's finally Susannah's turn. Even though we're all going to miss her around here, we understand why she's leaving. She deserves to have her moment in the sun."

Kane thought of the woman he had met. No wonder she was so strong. So determined. So invested in her sister's welfare. "She's never gone anywhere? College?"

"Susannah has never taken so much as a vacation. That girl has made Jackie her life." A tender smile took over Pastor Weatherly's face. "I can tell you care about Susannah, but remember everyone here in Chapel Ridge does, too. Whatever you do, do it in her best interests." He rose, laying a firm hand on Kane's shoulders before disappearing into the back of the church.

A rock of guilt sank to the pit of Kane's gut. Had Pastor Weatherly peeked inside Kane's conscience? Not five minutes before arriving at the church, Kane had been considering his exit strategy. Get out, get back to New York before he got any more wrapped up in this town, or Susannah Wilson. Staying in Chapel Ridge any longer than absolutely necessary would be a mistake. He saw no way to have both his life in New York and Susannah Wilson.

Except...

She wanted to explore the world, to leave this town. Maybe they could continue this on his turf, if she'd consider making New York City part of her itinerary.

One pesky problem remained. He had lied to her from

the moment he met her. Undoing that was nearly impossible, not without bringing him the very thing he didn't want, not quite yet.

A return to his regular life.

Or worse, the look of betrayal in Susannah's green eyes. He might not know Susannah Wilson very well, but he knew one thing. She valued honesty above everything else.

And a woman like Susannah could never love a man who lied.

"How'd it go?" Jackie said. "Sorry I'm late."

Susannah swiped at her face and turned around, grateful night had fallen and would mask her tears. "Fine."

"Were you crying just now?" Jackie leaned in close, peering at Susannah's face.

"No." Her voice betrayed her, hooking on the last syllable.

"You *were* crying." Jackie's voice lowered in sympathy. "Why?"

"I…I miss Mom, that's all. I started thinking about her missing the ceremony and it got me upset." There was a lot more emotion mixed up in those tears. Feelings about lost chances and the last few days, but Susannah kept that to herself. Instead, she reached out to her sister, clasping Jackie's hand and giving it a squeeze. "That was a really nice touch, you adding the hymn."

A smile trembled on Jackie's lips. "I wanted to surprise you. I thought you'd like it, too."

A look of understanding passed between them, of shared grief. How long had it been since the two of them had connected? On a sister level, not on a pseudo mother/daughter level? Susannah's heart swelled near to bursting. "It'll be beautiful, Jackie. Mom would have loved it."

Jackie sniffled, then rubbed her arms against the night chill. "Did the rehearsal work out all right otherwise?"

"Yep. Pastor Weatherly has a funeral in a little while, so Kane and I walked through the ceremony." Susannah didn't tell Jackie about the experience of standing at the front of the church and "marrying" Kane. About how real it had been. How...nice. How terrifying. For a moment at least, she'd forgotten what a completely insane idea marrying Kane would be. Then she'd come to her senses, thank goodness, and gotten out of there before things went any further. "I can go over the details if you want."

Jackie waved a hand. "Tomorrow morning is soon enough. Tonight, it's time to party." She grinned. "Remember, we're all meeting over at the Corner Kitchen for the rehearsal dinner? The pay-for-yourself rehearsal dinner, because Paul and I are poor, *and* we're saving our money for retirement."

Kane had gotten through to Jackie, on the financial end. Thank goodness. Nevertheless, even though Susannah had told her sister the rehearsal had made her upset because it made her miss her mother, she had really been more unsettled by Kane. She couldn't imagine sitting across from him at the Corner Kitchen tonight and acting as if nothing had happened, after just standing at the altar and hearing him feign a forever pledge. "Jackie, I'm not in much of a party mood."

"You always say that." Jackie let out a gust. "Susannah, why won't you just go? It'll be fun."

"You go. You have fun." Susannah started toward her car. "I'll go home and start the thank-you cards for the bridal shower gifts—"

Jackie grabbed her sleeve and stopped Susannah in her tracks. "No. Don't."

"You won't have time, Jackie. You know how disorganized you get with those things. And plus, you'll be back at work right after the honeymoon, and—"

"Susannah, I *want* you to have fun tonight." Jackie toed at the grass, tracing a half circle before raising her gaze to her sister's. "This is my wedding, and *I* should be doing these things."

Jackie had said the very same thing a dozen times before. Made promises she hadn't kept. Susannah shook her head. "Like being at your own rehearsal?"

"Yeah, like that."

Susannah bit her lip, refusing to get angry, to have an argument over this. "It's fine. I took care of it."

"That's the problem, Susannah. You're always taking care of me. And I let you, because it's so damned easy." Jackie turned away and crossed to a curved wrought iron bench beneath a magnolia tree. She took a seat, bracing her hands on either side, and swung her legs back and forth, leaving deep indents in the grass. "When I got to the church tonight and found out everyone was gone, and that you had already taken care of the rehearsal, I was…mad. Even though it was my fault."

"Jackie, what did you want me to do?" Susannah threw up her hands. "You weren't here. As usual. I had to do something."

"That wasn't why I was mad. I was mad at myself. For missing something I really wanted to be at. I know, I know, I did it to myself. It seems like every time I have good intentions, I do the wrong thing."

Susannah knew she could take the opportunity to jump on Jackie for all the mistakes of the past. Point out her faults, the areas where her younger sister had taken advantage. What would be the point? She'd rather hang tight to that thread of connection they'd begun to build tonight, and knit an even thicker rope. "You try, Jackie. And you're trying harder now."

"It's not enough. Not yet. I'm trying to get my life together, Suzie-Q, but you make it too easy for me not to."

Susannah rubbed at her temples. "What is that supposed to mean?"

Jackie took Susannah's hand and pulled her onto the bench beside her. She hesitated so long before speaking, Susannah wondered if Jackie would just brush off the conversation like she always did, with a joke or a distraction. Instead, she drew in a long breath, then let it out. "Ever since Mom and Dad died, you've taken good care of me. Really good care."

"That's my job, sis. I didn't want you to have to live with strangers or with some relatives in Arizona that we hardly knew."

"I know, but when I got older, you just *kept on* taking care of me." Jackie looked down at her hands. "And I let you. Because, well, I was lazy."

Susannah started to disagree. And stopped.

"I let you do everything for me, including my wedding. I shouldn't have done that." She took in a breath, let it out. "I don't want to miss any more of my wedding, Suzie. It's my wedding, not yours, and I'll only have the one. So, you are officially fired as my helper." She met Susannah's eyes and grinned.

"Fired?"

"Yep. From now on, all I want you to do is be my sister. And my maid of honor. That means, just show up tomorrow night and hold my bouquet when I'm at the altar."

Susannah leaned back against the bench, studying her sister. "What's with this sudden change of heart? I mean, I'm all for it, but—"

"Don't use that word. *But*. I'm working on being more responsible, and while I bet I'm going to screw up a lot, I'm going to try really hard. When you say 'but,' it's like you already doubt me." A tentative smile spread across Jackie's face, one that said she had her own doubts about herself but she was holding tight to her confidence. "Okay?"

"Okay." Jackie was grown up, and Susannah wanted to cry, both happy and sad, and full of love that threatened to burst from her heart. Her sister finally appreciated her, and understood what she had done—and now wanted to spread her own wings. Susannah leaned forward and drew Jackie into a tight hug. Jackie's arms went around Susannah's back, and the two of them embraced, the thread weaving together finally, bringing two sisters together again. Susannah's throat closed, and the tears spilled over, onto Jackie's shoulder. She cupped her sister's head. "Mom and Dad would be really proud of you," she whispered.

"No, Susannah," Jackie said softly, her voice hoarse. "They'd be really proud of you. Just as proud as I am that you're my sister." She drew back and their watery gazes met. "Thank you."

And with those two words, the bridge between them was finally healed.

The envelope had been a warning. The only person who had a contact address for Kane—his personal assistant, Laura—had sent the overnight message to warn him that his father had pulled out all the stops to find his son. Kane paid Laura well enough that he doubted she would talk, and either way, he hadn't given even her specific information. Just in case.

But it was only a matter of time. His father was not a man who would be denied anything, especially access to his son.

Kane paced the small cabin, Bandit running circles around his legs, unnerved by his temporary owner's continual movements. So much for a vacation. Four short days and already reality was dragging him back kicking and screaming.

Maybe it was a good thing. After all, twelve hours ago he'd been standing at the front of a church, before a minister, pledging to love Susannah till death did them part.

He had definitely *not* come here for that.

Except that moment hadn't been so bad. Or frightening. Or any of the other adjectives Kane had always associated with the thought of marriage. Maybe he could find a way to have it all. Or at least take baby steps in that direction.

For now, though, he had the envelope to deal with.

Kane crossed to the hearth and started a fire, this time with quick success. Susannah had shown him how to use a bit of newspaper to help the kindling catch the flame, then add the logs a little at a time, as well as how to operate the flue. Give him a few more days and he'd be a regular Grizzly Adams.

Bandit padded over to the fireplace and settled down at Kane's feet. Kane reached out and tousled the dog's ears. Bandit sighed and leaned into Kane's leg, tail beating a drum of happiness against the wood floor. "You like me?"

Bandit wagged some more.

He ran his hand down the dog's neck, patting the silky hair. "I've never had a dog, you know."

That apparently didn't bother Bandit, who wagged harder.

"I heard you're spoiled."

The dog whimpered a disagreement.

When he left, he'd be leaving the dog behind. Could he do that? Could he just pick up and go, and become the same old Kane Lennox again?

Did he even want to?

Kane's gaze traveled to the overnight envelope on the table.

Did he have a choice?

CHAPTER ELEVEN

"Isn't it a little early in the morning for alcohol?" Kane settled on the bar stool inside Flanagan's Pub beside Paul and ordered a coffee, waving off Paul's offer of a beer.

"I'm getting married today, Kane. *Married*." Paul gripped the beer bottle like a life preserver. "Am I insane?"

"Do you love her?"

"Of course I do."

"Then no, you're not insane. At least not entirely." Kane grinned.

"Ha, ha." Paul took a deep gulp of the beer, made a face, then pushed the brown bottle to the side. "You're right. It is too early in the morning for beer."

Kane chuckled and signaled for a second cup of coffee. The bartender shook his head at the two men as he slid the steaming mugs across the bar. Kane thanked him. As the bartender walked away to finish drying glasses, Kane pulled out his wallet for some bills and laid enough money on the oak surface to cover the coffee and a generous tip. Kane turned back to Paul. "Did you and Jackie work everything out?"

"Kane, what are you doing?"

"Sitting here, talking to you…" Kane flicked out his

wrist. "At nine in the morning, in a bar. Reminds me of our college days."

"I meant with that." Paul gestured toward the tip, then leaned forward and lowered his voice to a whisper. "In this town, we don't leave a bartender a hundred-dollar tip. The guy is going to have a coronary when he sees that."

"Oh. You told me about what happened with his family…how he's been struggling. I know a hundred bucks isn't going to make much difference, but it should at least make his day."

Paul leaned back on his bar stool, his jaw slack. "You are *not* the same guy I knew in college."

"What, just because I'm drinking coffee instead of beer in the morning? All of us grow up, Paul. I bet you cut back, too. You have a job. Teaching kids, at that. Can't show up at school drunk or hung over, I'm sure."

"I'm not talking about the drinking. I'm talking about this…" he waved a hand over Kane "…this socially conscious, socially involved Kane."

He chuckled. "You make me sound like the next step up from Cro-Magnon Man."

"You are, compared to the rest of us guys."

Larry headed over, a pot of coffee in one hand. He started to refill Kane's mug when he spied the money, and froze. "Whoa! Dude, is that a hundred-dollar bill?"

"Yep." Kane grinned. "And it's for you."

The stout, tall man stared at the green paper. Then at Kane, then back again at the hundred dollars. "Uh…you only got coffee."

Kane smiled. "I know."

The bartender held the bill up to the light, as if he still couldn't believe it was real. "You sure? Is this really for me?"

"The whole thing. Take your wife out for dinner, pay

some bills. Relieve some stress." Kane leaned forward. "I know all about needing to relieve stress. Hope that helps."

"Yeah, it will. Thanks. I mean, *thanks*." The bartender backed up and reached for the wall phone, then started dialing. "Honey, you aren't going to believe this…"

As Larry chatted with his wife, Kane's heart swelled. Damn. Who knew giving could feel this great? And all he'd done was overtip.

Kane returned his attention to Paul. "That felt good. I mean, I give plenty of money to charities every year, but that's writing a check. This was hands-on. Maybe I should start handing out money on the street to perfect strangers."

Paul arched a brow. "Are you dying or something?"

"No. Just…" Kane drew in a breath, and when he did, he swore he could catch the floral notes of Susannah's perfume. She'd rubbed off on him, that was for sure. She and the rest of this small town. "Just enjoying my life for the first time ever."

"Well, if handing over money makes you feel good…" Paul grinned, then put up his hands. "Just kidding, buddy. I never liked you for your money, you know that."

"I do. And I appreciate it." Kane gave Paul a good-natured clap on the back. He had thought of giving his friend a healthy check for a wedding present but decided a more-personal gift—one that meant something to Kane himself—would be far better. He reached into the breast pocket of his leather jacket and pulled out an envelope. "I want you and Jackie to have this."

"What…" Paul's voice trailed off, caught in a breath. He held the envelope tight, reading the name of the travel agency on the front, then the word Jamaica beneath the logo. "*Jamaica?* But, Kane, we can't—"

"You can and you will. Life's too short, Paul. I know

you guys are tight on money and you were planning just a simple three-day honeymoon in Chicago. Nothing against that city, but you two deserve more, especially for your honeymoon. I talked to your principal and to Jackie's boss, and got you a few more days off. Two weeks, to be exact."

"Two weeks?" Paul's eyes widened. "How the hell did you manage that?"

"I, uh, offered to pay for the substitute. The principal was arguing about the cost of that until I said I'd pony up the cash. Seems small towns have small budgets when it comes to substitute teachers."

"Small towns have small budgets for everything, Kane." Paul turned the envelope over in his hand, staring at it, incredulous. "You have got to be kidding me. This is too much." Then he shook his head and slid the envelope across the bar. "We can't accept it."

Kane slid it back to Paul. "You saved my ass in college a dozen times. This is just a small way to repay you, to say thanks."

"Hey, all I did was help you study for some tests."

"No. You helped me have a life. Outside the Lennox name. That saved my sanity. Down the road it brought me here, and that saved me a second time."

"I call it even, Kane, after you talked to Jackie and convinced her saving money will make her a millionaire." Paul grinned. "Heck, I would have been happy just to have Jackie see the value of a savings account, but you've got her talking 401ks and 529s for our kids. You're a miracle worker."

Kane chuckled, then sobered. "I found something in Chapel Ridge, Paul, that taught me a lesson. Something I wanted to share with you. That's what this is really about." Kane cupped his hands around his coffee and stared into the dark liquid. "The years will pass so fast, Paul, your head will spin, and you'll wish you took the days off when you could. So do it now, while someone else is footing the tab."

Paul opened his mouth to protest again, then stopped. "Okay. But only because Jackie would kill me if I said no."

Kane laughed. "Good."

"What about you?"

"What about me?"

"Are you just going to go back to being Kane Lennox, or are you going to have a life when you get back to New York?"

Kane snorted. "You know my father, Paul. What do you think? Nothing will make him happy but me being at work twenty-four hours a day."

"Why do you try so hard?" Paul asked. "I don't want to tell you how to live your life, but why do you worry so much about what your father thinks?"

Kane spun the coffee mug back and forth. "It's complicated. He's not a bad man, just…difficult."

Paul bit his lip, closing the subject of Kane's father. "What are you going to do about Susannah?"

"Do? Nothing."

Paul snorted. "Right. I heard from my groomsmen what happened at the altar last night. Seems you two have a few feelings for each other. They said they felt like they were watching a real wedding."

Kane's mind rocketed back to that moment, to Susannah, standing beneath the jeweled light of the stained glass. To her smile when he pledged his love. Real or not, for a moment, it had been believable. Then she had run out of there, and avoided the rehearsal dinner. Avoided him. Making it clear that what had happened at that altar hadn't been real to her. Or if it had been, it had been a real nightmare. "Well, we were just acting."

Paul gave him a light elbow jab. "Maybe you're in the

wrong industry. Everyone in the pews said it was worthy of an Academy Award."

Kane thought again of the envelope. Of the warning from his assistant. His father would never approve of Susannah, and that would leave the two Lennox men even more divided than they already were. How could that do any of them, or for that matter, the company, any good? "And maybe I just need to remember my place."

Beneath the family yoke.

"Reggie is sure going to miss you," Cecilia Richards said, taking her Pomeranian from Susannah and giving the freshly groomed, caramel-colored dog a cuddle. "Are you sure I can't talk you into staying in town? Where else will I find a groomer who's as patient with my sweet little boy as you are?"

Susannah smiled. Mrs. Richards's "sweet little boy" had a temperament that usually required a muzzle and hazardous-duty pay. The Pomeranian had a hatred of all things water, and made his displeasure about his baths well known from the minute he arrived at The Sudsy Dog. Tess refused to go near him. Susannah had always been the only one who could calm Reggie enough to get him through the experience. "I'll miss him, too," she said, giving Reggie a pat and a little treat. The Pom wagged his tail, probably out of relief that the ordeal was finally over.

"You *are* coming back, aren't you? You aren't going to go to the other side of the world and stay there?"

Susannah sighed. "Yes, I'm coming back. In three weeks." As much as she didn't want to return, her bank account was only so deep, and what would be left after her trip to Paris was needed for an apartment rental.

"Oh, good." Mrs. Richards gave her dog a little nuzzling

kiss, then pouted. "But who will take care of my Reggie until then?"

"Tess would be glad to." Tess would kill her for saying that, but the girl had agreed to take any emergency appointments while Susannah was gone. The shelter dogs had all been adopted or fostered for Susannah's absence. Virtually every last detail had been attended to. Her suitcase was packed. Her last appointment was leaving, thanking her one more time as she got in her car with a growling, barking Reggie. All Susannah had left to do was clean up the shop, make her last deposit, and lock the doors.

Then after the wedding tonight, she was free. Free to finally live her own life. Free to fulfill the dream her mother and father had never had a chance to see.

As Mrs. Richards and Reggie pulled away, Susannah headed back inside The Sudsy Dog. She turned the shop sign to Closed and went into the washing room. In a few minutes, she had the tub cleaned, the supplies put away and everything put in order.

She hung up her apron and looked around at the silent rooms. She was done.

Her gaze strayed to the Arc de Triomphe poster. Tomorrow night, she would be there. Stand in that very city, seeing those sights. But for the first time since Susannah had made the decision to go to Paris, the thought didn't fill her with the same sense of joy.

"Paris is a beautiful city, especially in springtime."

She whirled around and found Kane standing behind her. Dark jeans hugged his hips, outlined his powerful legs, while a white button-down shirt stretched across his chest, beneath a black leather jacket. He'd left a couple of buttons undone, enough to give her a teasing view of the chest she knew existed beneath. A crazy part of Susannah wanted to undo every last button, place her hands against his skin, and do what she hadn't done that day in the laundry room. Feel him beneath her. Taste his skin. And take this beyond a couple of passionate kisses. "What are you doing here? I thought you'd be with Paul today."

"I was, but he's all set for a while." Kane closed the gap between them, his purposeful strides making quick work of the small room. His gaze connected with hers, and the temperature seemed to rise, the tension in the room double. "He had his doubts about long-term commitment, but they passed."

Doubts. She'd had those ever since she'd met Kane Lennox. Doubts about who he was. Why he was here. Whether she should get involved with him. And now, doubts about whether she would forget him once she left town. For a woman who hadn't wanted to leave behind any strings, she suddenly felt very tied to this man.

Most of the lights in the shop were off, leaving only the late-afternoon sun's rays. The last golden light of the day cast a romantic veil over the room, washing Kane with soft highlights, almost like he, too, were part of the scenery that hung on her walls.

"That happens." Were they even talking about Paul and Jackie? Desire coiled in Susannah's gut. She tightened her hold on the brush in her hand, twisting the handle against her palm.

Kane closed the gap. His gaze dropped to her mouth, then back to her eyes. "He realized he didn't want to go on without her."

"Good." The word escaped her on a breath.

"What happened to you last night?" Kane asked.

"I didn't want to go to the party. I, um, wasn't feeling well." Liar. She'd felt fine. She'd been disconcerted by him. By what had happened back in the church. And really afraid it would show on her face when he looked at her in the restaurant.

"You know what I mean." He tipped her jaw. "What happened at that altar?"

"We…" Her voice trailed off. Why lie? Why pretend? They both knew something had shifted last night, something big. "That was more than just acting, wasn't it?"

He nodded. Slowly. "I know we don't know each other well. And I know how insane that sounds. But you are the first woman I have ever met who sees me for me. Just me. And that—" he smiled "—is the sexiest thing I've ever experienced."

Her heart trilled, her pulse raced. She tried to keep the feelings tamped down, away from showing. "Well, that saves me from wearing high heels."

He laughed, then drew her into his arms. "I mean it, Susannah. You are…everything I always wanted and never even knew existed."

Now the emotion burst onto Susannah's face in a wide smile. Her arms went around Kane, and he drew her to him. She fit against him perfectly, like a lost diamond fitting into its setting. Beneath his shirt, she heard his heartbeat, the steady thump-thump matching her own. "You found that here, in Chapel Ridge, Indiana? And not in New York?"

"Exactly." He leaned down and brushed his lips against hers, tender and sweet, a slow, easy kiss. "But I don't want to lose this. I…I want you to come to New York with me. Right after the wedding."

She backed up, out of his embrace. "What?"

"Come to New York with me. I can rent you an apartment, rent you space for dogs and cats." He grinned. "Whatever you want."

New York City. The epicenter of the country, where everything happened, all the activity came in and went out. She'd be out of this small town forever. Away from its expectations, away from her responsibilities.

But…would she be trading up? Or trading laterally?

She replayed his words in her head, and heard the empty pockets in the sentences. Had he left those gaps on purpose, or was she simply missing something?

"I don't want that, Kane," Susannah said. "I want… more."

"What? A house? That can be arranged. A car? I'll take care of it."

Things. He was offering her *things*. Every single tangible item—

Except his heart.

"No, Kane. I don't want you to pay for me. For one, it's too expensive—"

"I can afford it, I assure you."

"For another, I want to achieve something big, on my own. I want…" She searched for the words she had yet to find, had yet to have time to find. "I want to see the world. Be my own person. Get out from under the shadow of Chapel Ridge. Of being the older Wilson sister. I can't do that if you're funding my move and my life." She drew in a breath and met his gaze. "I don't want to be something you treat like a pet you're boarding at an apartment nearby. If I'm living with a man, I want it to be because I *married* him."

He turned and let out a low curse. "You want everything."

"It's my right, isn't it? To want a full life? And what's wrong with that?"

"I can't give you everything. I have…expectations of my own."

"What kind of expectations could there possibly be,

Kane? I mean, you told me you work in a jewelry store, right? I understand if you work long hours and don't have a lot of time to devote to a relationship. That's, like, the story of my life."

He didn't meet her gaze. Susannah should have taken that as the first sign, but she didn't. That silly bird of hope kept trying to fly in her chest. "It's more than that. My job is beyond demanding. And that has to come first."

"Work comes first?" she repeated, dumbfounded. "This from the man who has been lecturing me all week about taking time off to have a life of my own?"

"I'd be offering you a life, Susannah. A different one from what you have here."

And then she knew. There was no possibility of this dream ever taking flight. A bittersweet smile curved across Susannah's face, and disappointment sank heavy and sour in her stomach. She'd thought she'd known him, but it turned out Kane Lennox had been a stranger all along. "Tell me what the difference is, Kane. In New York, you'd simply be paying me to be with you instead of paying me to teach you to fish."

She rose on her tiptoes and gave him a quick kiss on the cheek, then turned and walked out of The Sudsy Dog. Before she could change her mind and take what he was offering.

Which, really, was nothing she wanted.

CHAPTER TWELVE

THE stretch black limo pulled up in front of The Sudsy Dog, drawing Susannah up short. Except for the occasional funeral, prom or wedding rental, limos never drove through Chapel Ridge. And they never stopped in downtown, in front of the dog-grooming salon.

"Susannah, wait!" Kane called after her, exiting The Sudsy Dog fast on her heels.

She didn't want to stop. Didn't want to deal with anyone, not when her heart was breaking and all she wanted was to retreat to the solitude of her home.

As Kane caught up to her, his hand touching her arm lightly to keep her from leaving, a well-dressed man stepped out of the luxury car. Susannah heard Kane curse under his breath, and realized this was no ordinary limo. And no ordinary visitor.

The man in the suit had distaste and barely restrained fury written all over his features. He buttoned his jacket as he walked toward Kane, not saying a word, simply glaring. First at Kane, then including Susannah, too.

"What a surprise," Kane said, his body language reading the exact opposite. "Susannah, this is my father, Elliott Lennox." This man was Kane's *father?* What was he doing here? And in that car? Beside her, Kane had gone tense, on guard. "Father, this is—"

"Don't act like you don't know why I'm here," the other man cut in, as sharp as a razor. He turned to Susannah and a charming smile took over his face. If she hadn't just seen it herself, she'd think the earlier fury was imagined. There were layers here—layers between the two men, layers in the two men—that Susannah couldn't see. "Excuse me, miss, but this is between my son and me. If you could give us a moment?"

Everything about Elliott Lennox screamed "get away," even with the polite smile. Susannah had no desire to stand in the middle of this tense standoff, and was about to step away when Kane put his hand on her arm again. "No, she won't," he said, his tone just as sharp, insistent.

Elliott scowled. "Kane, don't drag some vacation dalliance into the middle of our family business."

Vacation dalliance? The words hit Susannah like a verbal slap. She opened her mouth to tell him off, when she remembered her place. Downtown Chapel Ridge was neither the time nor the place to stage a scene with Kane's father.

"Don't call her that." Kane's tone was even, controlled, but a growlish undertone lay beneath his words. "Susannah deserves your respect."

Elliott let out a breath of impatience and ran a hand through his silver hair. He had the same height and similar bearing to Kane, but everything else about him, from his clear disdain for the town to his instant hatred of her, seemed like he had DNA from a whole other country. "Enough of this. You've had your fun, now come back to work. For God's sake, you can't keep carrying on like this. What do you think the media will say if they find out you're here in the backwoods, living like a heathen?"

"Mr. Lennox," Susannah cut in, "Chapel Ridge is a small town, certainly nothing that would create some media firestorm for anyone on vacation. And I can't believe the jewelry store can't live without Kane for a few days."

A smirk took over Elliott's face. "Is that what you've told people around here? That you work in a *jewelry store?*" He took a step away from his son and toward Susannah. "Don't you know who he is?"

Kane's eyes narrowed. "Don't."

"This man is Kane Lennox, of the Lennox Gem—"

"I'm warning you."

"Corporation," Elliott went on, ignoring his son. "He is one of the richest men in the world, CEO of one of the biggest companies in the world. That is, if I and the rest of the board don't decide to fire him for this little embarrassment he put us through." Elliott waved at her as if she alone comprised the embarrassment he mentioned.

Then the sentences began to assemble in Susannah's mind. Kane Lennox. CEO. Lennox Gem Corporation.

One of *the* Lennoxes.

Not a jewelry store worker at all.

Susannah's jaw dropped and she stared at Kane, who started to voice an explanation, then stopped when he read her expression. The words added up, one at a time, building blocks suddenly forming into a recognizable shape. Everything Kane had said over the last few days. All the half-truths he'd told, the way he'd acted, the way he'd seemed out of place.

And then his offer—

His offer to put her up in an apartment in New York. His "vacation dalliance," taken back home to the big city. As what, his mistress? While he married some society beauty, someone who would help him expand his corporate reach?

"You...you bastard," she said, the betrayal hitting hard, slicing through her heart. "How could you?"

"Susannah, I have an explanation."

"You lied to me. Everything you said was a lie."

"Not everything, no."

"Oh, did he tell you he loved you? Or make you some ridiculous promise?" Elliott said, then snorted. "Please, Kane, don't toy with people like that. Let this poor woman be. She'd never fit in with your life and you know it." Elliott crossed to the limo and opened the door. "I'm getting back in the car. If you were smart, you would, too."

Elliott did as he said, leaving the limo door open. Waiting for Kane and his decision. Go back to New York, leaving Susannah behind. And forget this silly vacation dalliance forever.

She waited. For Kane to turn around. For him to look at her and tell her his father was wrong. That he would stay here, with her. Because she was more important than anything else. Because he loved her, and he would sacrifice anything to have her in his life.

But he didn't turn around, and he didn't say any of those things.

Susannah's heart shattered. She spun on her heel and ran to her car. Pulling away, she refused to look in her rearview mirror. She couldn't even if she'd wanted to. The tears blurred her vision.

The candles flickered in the church, bathing the room in a soft, golden glow. A hundred guests filled the pews, chatting quietly among themselves while they waited.

Susannah closed the double doors, then ducked back into the bridal room. "Everything's all set."

Jackie stood in front of the full-length mirror, adjusting

her veil, then smoothing the front of her simple spaghetti-strap, tea-length dress. "I thought I'd be nervous, but I'm not."

Susannah drew her younger sister into a one-armed hug, careful not to crinkle the satin cap sleeves and bodice of her light blue maid-of-honor dress. "That's because you're marrying Mr. Right."

Jackie smiled. "Paul is pretty wonderful, isn't he?"

"Yep." A little shiver of melancholy ran through Susannah. Her sister was marrying the right guy, beginning the rest of her life with him, and Susannah should be over-joyed for Jackie. And she was—

But she was also envious, in a weird way. Only because of that betrayal with Kane earlier. How could he have lied to her? After all they'd talked about and shared? She'd told him so much about herself, and he'd made up every-thing he'd told her.

Even what he felt? Had each kiss been a fraud, too?

A sharp ache ran through her chest, and tears threatened again at Susannah's eyes. She heard Kane's offer of an apartment in New York, followed by Elliott's taunting, as if he'd caught Kane doing that a hundred times before. Just one more vacation dalliance.

How stupid could she be?

"Susannah? Are you paying attention? I needed help with the straps on my shoes."

"Oh, sure." Susannah took a seat on an ottoman and bent to slip the straps into the tiny gold buckles.

"Are you all right? You're so distracted."

She rose. "Just thinking about all those last-minute de-tails before I get on the plane tomorrow."

Jackie took Susannah's hand, her eyes misty. "I wish you weren't going away."

"I'll be back." She'd return to Chapel Ridge, to her life.

To her business. And to a decidedly empty feeling, after all that had happened with Kane. Susannah brushed the emotion away. A few weeks in Paris would help her forget.

It would.

"I know. But I'm going to miss you all the same. We've never been apart."

"We haven't, have we?" Susannah gave Jackie's hand a squeeze. "Don't worry. I'll call you every day."

"You better." Jackie swiped at her face. "Though I don't know if I'll have cell service in Jamaica."

"Jamaica?" Susannah blinked. "I thought you were going to Chicago."

"I didn't tell you?" Jackie drew back, beaming with joy. "Kane did the sweetest thing. He called my boss, and Paul's, and got us both two weeks off, then gave us a trip to Jamaica as a wedding present."

"Wow! That's generous." She chided herself for being surprised. He was a millionaire after all, probably even a billionaire. A trip to Jamaica was a drop in the ocean of money to a guy like him.

Hadn't he just proved to her that money was more important than people? In the end, he'd go back to his billion-dollar life. Who could blame him, really? When his choice was staying here with the fishing poles and stray dogs?

"Paul asked Kane why he did it," Jackie went on, "and he said that he wanted us to experience what he did while he was here in Chapel Ridge. He said he found something here he never found anywhere else." Jackie turned to the table, picked up her bouquet, then checked her reflection one more time. "What kind of experience does *anyone* have in Chapel Ridge? I mean, this has to be the most boring town in the country."

"Yeah. Nothing to offer here." Susannah pretended to

check her own reflection, the long blond hair, the plainer of the two Wilson sisters, avoiding Jackie's gaze, avoiding the truth about Kane and his "experiences," then pivoted away from the mirror. "It's almost time to go, Jackie. In a little while you'll be married to Paul."

"I can only do that," Jackie said with a smile, "if you get ready to walk down that aisle first. Can't get married without my sister standing by me, now can I?"

The only trouble? Susannah already knew who else would be waiting at the end of that aisle. And she wasn't so sure she could face him ever again.

CHAPTER THIRTEEN

IN THE PAST HOUR, KANE had been fired, disowned and written out of the Lennox family will. Twice. Now his father was trying the silent treatment. Didn't matter. Kane refused to be dissuaded. "I'm not going back to New York, not this second anyway."

Elliott Lennox didn't respond. He stood in Kane's rustic kitchen, as still as a statue. His silver hair and regal bearing made him look like a piece of art, particularly against the roughly hewn cabin's backdrop.

"I'm the best man, and that means I honor my commitment. You'd want me to do that, wouldn't you?"

Again, his father said nothing.

Kane shook his head. "What's it going to take? What do I have to do to get your attention? To get you to acknowledge me as your son?"

Elliott wheeled around. "When you start *acting* like my son, that's when I'll acknowledge you."

"Tell me a day when I didn't," Kane shot back.

"This week, for one." Elliott shook his head. "You abandoned your family. Your responsibilities. That is simply unacceptable. God, it's like you're back in college again and I need to clean up your mess."

"Is that what you're going to do? Ship Susannah off to Europe so I don't embarrass you again?"

"There was more involved than an embarrassment for the family, Kane."

Kane snorted. "What, was my involvement with Rebecca back in college going to affect some business deal for you? Her father had a one-percent stake in a competitor?"

"She wanted your money."

Kane rolled his eyes. "Right. And so does every other woman I date who you don't agree with. I swear, you'd handpick my ties if I let you."

Elliott toyed with the coffee mug before him. "Rebecca came to me over Christmas break. Walked right into my office, as bold as brass. Said she was going to marry you whether I liked it or not."

Kane chuckled. "That's Rebecca for you."

"Then she said I could stop the wedding for a quarter million dollars."

The blow to Kane's chest hit swift and hard. He stepped back, reaching for the back of a chair. "You're lying."

His father's gaze met his. "I never lie about money, Kane."

Kane thought back to how quickly Rebecca had disappeared from his life. How easy it had seemed for her to go, once she had received the buyout from his father, the offer of an overseas education. Disgust rose in his chest. "Did you pay her the money?"

"We came to an acceptable arrangement." Elliott took a sip of coffee, then held tight to the mug, not saying anything for a long time. "I was *protecting* you, Kane. You have a tendency to see the world through rose-colored glasses. You believe the best in people. I…I see them for what they are."

Kane let out a gust. "What, everyone is greedy?"

A slight smile crossed his father's face. "No. Not everyone is like you."

"Selfish and impetuous, is that it?"

"I can't say I've agreed with all your decisions, but you are more…trusting than I am. And there have been days when I wish I had some of your leap-off-the-bridge attitude."

The words took Kane by surprise. A compliment from his father—as rare as spotting a saltwater marlin in the middle of the Indiana lake. His anger dissipated, and he moved closer, seeing Elliott with new, less-jaded eyes. "You never thought of just simply taking off on a vacation? Running away from it all for a day or two? Or a week?"

"We all have those thoughts. But I had too much on my shoulders to ever indulge in them. My father, the company, your mother, you."

Kane shook his head. "You could have taken time off."

"And who would have run Lennox? Who would have made sure my father stayed in line? He might as well have been a child, given how little attention he paid to the business. To the rest of us. He spent more time at the gambling table than at the office. Someone had to step up, Kane, and that someone was me. Then I was married, a father, and years later, I had a sick wife. I had no time for flights of fancy or otherwise."

Understanding began to pour into Kane's blood. He thought back over the years, and finally saw his father's life, realizing all those hours at the office hadn't been a choice, they'd been a duty. Not to the company that bore his name, but to his family. "I had no idea."

Elliott shrugged. "I wasn't going to burden you with my problems."

"You should have. It would have helped me understand you."

Elliott shook his head. "Neither of us understands the other very well, do we? We've always been at odds. Like two bulldogs."

Kane studied the wood floor, memorizing the grain of the long, straight boards, before speaking words that had lain within him for a long time, festering. It was time he got it all out. Shared the reasons he had left New York. "I was wrong for leaving without a word, or at least answering my cell phone. The fish have it now." His father's brows knitted in confusion, but Kane went on. "I feel like I've spent my life trying to live up to some impossible standard. To please you, to do everything you've asked of me. Today is the first time you've ever complimented me, that I can remember. You treat your employees better then your own son."

"I gave you the best things in life. The best home, food, clothes, schools. Gave you a job."

"I didn't *want* any of that!" Kane swallowed the rest of his temper, then turned away and crossed to the cold fireplace.

"What did you want? A better car? Bigger house?" Elliott let out a frustrated gust. "A raise? I pay you well enough."

Kane rested his grip on the mantel, clutching the stones above the fireplace, their hard solidity providing strength. "I wanted you," he said softly. "That was all."

The room fell silent. A chair screeched, then creaked.

Kane turned around, and found his father at the table, looking older than he ever had before. His face seemed to have added wrinkles, his shoulders seemed to droop.

"You *had* me, Kane. Every day. I came home after work. And then, when you were done with college, you went to work for me. How can you say that I wasn't there?"

Kane crossed to the table, and sank into the opposite chair. "You were, but not as a father. All I wanted was the occasional hug. A few *atta-boys* here and there. Would it have been so hard to say, 'Hey, Kane, I'm proud of you,' instead of 'don't embarrass the family again'?"

Elliott turned away. "You know how I feel. I'm not some touchy-feely guy. For God's sake, that's no way to do business."

"A family is not a business, Father."

Elliott ran a hand over his face. He sat there a long time, so long, Kane was afraid he had gone back to the silent treatment. Then he swallowed hard and let out a breath before facing his son. "You know who used to say that to me all the time? My mother. She'd remind me, over and over, that family wasn't business. She told my father, too, but he didn't listen any more than I did, I guess. You get…consumed, Kane."

"Like Uncle Harold."

"That man worked himself to death. Died on the job, for God's sake." Elliott shook his head. "Should have had the sense to retire when he had a chance."

Kane arched a brow. "Know anybody like that?"

"I'm nothing like my brother." Elliott paused. "I simply haven't found anything better I want to do than go to work."

"Spend time with your family?"

"What family? You're all grown up. Your mother is…" His gaze drifted off, and Kane knew then another major reason why Elliott had poured himself into the company. "Is gone."

He looked at his father, a man he knew better as the chairman of the board than as a patriarch, and felt his heart soften. This could have been him, in a few years, if he hadn't run away to Chapel Ridge for a few days. If he hadn't taken time to walk a stray dog, dig in the earth, walk barefoot on the grass. "But *I'm* still here, Father. It's not too late, you know. You're not Uncle Harold. You still have time."

Elliott ran a hand over the cup of coffee before him, a

cup he had topped off earlier with a little bit of scotch. "Time for you and me?"

An olive branch. Kane would take it and hold on tight. If he'd learned one thing in his time in Chapel Ridge, it was that life was too damned short to waste it holding a grudge. "Do you like to fish?"

Elliott let out what might have been considered a laugh. "Fish? Are you serious?"

"As a stock report. If you want to hang around Chapel Ridge for a few days, I can show you the best fishing holes."

"Who would run the company?"

"That's the beauty of a huge company, Father. There are plenty of people to call on to take your place. Competent people that you and I hired. Trust them, and then go and relax. It'll do you a world of good."

Elliott let out a gust. "You're insane."

"No. I'm happy." Kane rose, then reached for the leash by the door and tossed it to his father. Elliott caught the lead and stared at his son. "Take some advice from a friend of mine and start with walking a dog. You might even want to try doing it barefoot. Spring grass is amazing under your feet."

"Walking a dog? You really are crazy. I can't possibly—"

"I thought the same thing. Bandit over there knows what to do. He'll lead you. And who knows…you might have fun." Kane grinned, grabbed the rental's car keys off the table, then grasped the door handle. He looked at his father, and thought about what had just transpired, and realized that he had nearly made the same mistakes as his father today. He'd tried to hold too tightly—and nearly lost everything he wanted. "I'll be back in a little while."

"Where are you going?"

"I have a wedding to go to. There's a guy I know who's

about to take the biggest risk of all, and get married, even though he makes hardly anything for money, and doesn't even have a five-year plan. He's doing it because he's in love. And if I play my cards right, I'll be doing the same thing really soon."

Then Kane hopped in his car and hurried down the lane toward the Chapel Ridge Lutheran Church, barely on time for the wedding. But hopefully not too late to get Susannah back.

Déjà vu.

Susannah stood at the front of the church, while Jackie and Paul were quiet and solemn at the altar in front of the minister, hands clasped, repeating the same words she had heard Kane say just last night. Had it been a mere twenty-four hours ago that the two of them had stood before Pastor Weatherly and rehearsed the wedding? Only a day since she believed, just for a moment, that maybe there was a future with this man?

She snuck a glance across the aisle at Kane. Her hormones betrayed her mind, jumping into action, raising her body temperature, accelerating her heartbeat. Apparently they hadn't gotten the memo that her mind was trying to forget Kane, because looking at him now brought desire roaring to the surface.

But appearances weren't everything, and she had to remind herself that this handsome package had come with a hefty package of falsehoods, too. He had lied to her, let her down and she couldn't forgive him for that.

Kane tried to catch her eye, sending her a smile, but Susannah turned her gaze away and refocused on the bridal couple.

"I now pronounce you husband and wife," Pastor

Weatherly said. He leaned in toward Paul. "You may kiss the bride."

Paul swooped Jackie into his arms, gave her a tender but passionate kiss, then pivoted her toward the church. Behind them, Pastor Weatherly introduced the new couple, and a moment later Mrs. Maxwell was playing the recessional as the several dozen guests applauded and wiped away tears.

Jackie and Paul swished down the aisle. Then Kane stepped onto the rose-covered path, his arm bent, and waited for Susannah. She pasted a smile on her face, slipped her arm into Kane's, and started walking. Just a few more minutes and this charade would be over.

Damn her body. His touch still sent a zing through her, still caused a reaction. Every ounce of her went on high alert—all those parts that had yet to forget what it felt like to be in Kane's arms. To have his lips on hers.

"You look beautiful," Kane whispered as they made their way to the back of the church.

"And you look like a liar," she snapped under her breath. She would not fall for him. Not again.

"Let me explain, Susannah."

They slipped past the double doors. As soon as they were outside the church, Susannah yanked her arm out of Kane's. "Why? You're leaving town anyway. Don't worry, Kane, I get it. You decided to fool around with the small-town girl, then leave her behind. Just one more memory in your vacation scrapbook, huh? Another *dalliance* to add to the tally?"

"It wasn't like that, Susannah."

"I heard exactly how it was, Kane *Lennox*." She headed down the granite steps of the church, unable to listen to another word. She waited on the sidewalk for the receiving line to finish, realizing then that she was stuck. She needed to ride to the reception with the rest of the bridal party, and right now, the bridesmaids were chatting it up inside the church. Just when Susannah needed to make a quick escape, too.

She was about to bum a ride off Mrs. Maxwell when a stretch white limo pulled up. A tall, thin chauffeur hopped out and opened the rear door. "Your car, miss?" he said to Susannah.

"Oh, no, this isn't for me. It's for the bride and groom."

"No, miss. This one is yours. There will be another one here shortly for them." The chauffeur waved again at the richly appointed interior of the limo—all leather, with a fully stocked bar, even a television.

"Mine? But…"

"It's yours, Susannah. I still owe you a tip," Kane said, coming up behind her, his hand at the small of her back, setting off those traitorous hormones again. "Please don't say no. The whole town is staring at you, waiting for something to gossip about anyway."

Susannah glanced over her shoulder and saw Kane was right. The guests who had turned out for Paul and Jackie's wedding—from Larry the bartender to Mrs. Maxwell—were all watching the exchange, and the unusual sight of a limo, followed by a second one rounding the corner, with undisguised interest. She had two choices. Stand here and let her business be known by all of Chapel Ridge, or get inside and at least keep the damage contained. Susannah climbed into the car, then slid over when Kane followed her.

The chauffeur shut the door, and in an instant, all of Chapel Ridge was muffled. The world closed in, becoming just her. And Kane.

"*Now* will you listen to me?" he asked.

"It seems I'm your hostage," she said, echoing his words

from a few days earlier, "for as long as it takes to get to the Chapel Ridge Hotel."

A grin curved across his mouth, then he leaned forward and brought his lips within a centimeter of hers. Her pulse raised, and anticipation pooled in her veins, warring with her better sense. "Then I better make good use of the time."

CHAPTER FOURTEEN

KANE didn't kiss Susannah, not exactly, even though every cell in his body screamed for him to. Instead, he drew back, allowing her distance and space, and prepared to plead his case. If he couldn't get her to listen in the next few miles, he'd lose her forever.

And that was the one price Kane Lennox, one of the richest men in the world, couldn't afford to pay.

"I'm sorry," he said.

She crossed her arms over her chest. Not budging an inch. "Why would you lie to me?"

"Because I wanted someone to look at me for me, not for my money. It was simple as that, Susannah."

"And what, you think so little of me that you don't think I could see past the money?"

"Past *billions* of dollars? Susannah, you're an incredible woman, but no one sees past that. Trust me. I know, because I've met dozens of people over the years and not a one looked at me and didn't see a dollar sign before my name."

She shook her head and turned to watch the town passing by the tinted windows. "I really don't think we have anything to say to each other, Kane. It's easier if you just leave me alone. We don't even have to talk to each other at the reception."

Kane ran a hand through his hair. He hadn't expected this to be easy, but knew, as the limo made another turn, that his time was running out. Small towns equaled short distances from one place to another. For the first time ever, he wished for the insane stop-and-go New York City traffic, which could have bought him a hefty half hour just to get from one side of Central Park to the other, given the right time of day.

Once the car stopped at the hotel, Susannah would bolt, and the chances of him having this kind of uninterrupted, captive audience time again were slim. "What are you going to do, Susannah, hop on that plane tomorrow and run away from the town, just like you're running away from me right now?"

She pivoted back. "I'm not running from anything. I'm going out on my own, having my life. That's not a crime."

He took her hand, running his fingers gently over the delicate bones. But she remained stiff, unyielding to his touch. "It is, if you're doing it so you can avoid the things in your life that scare you."

Her chin raised, defiant. "I'm not scared of anything."

"Oh, yeah?" With his free hand, he cupped her jaw, his touch against her cheek doing the same thing it had from the first time his palm had met her skin, offering a soothing balm to his soul. "You're scared of the same thing I am."

Her green eyes widened, their depths as rich as pure emeralds. Kane had worked with gems all his life, and never seen a single one as beautiful as the two in Susannah's gaze. "What's that?" The words were a breath.

"Falling in love. Giving up control to your emotions."

"I'm not—"

He pressed a finger to her lips, caught in the way the light blue of her dress set off the golden strands in her hair, accented the emerald in her gaze. His heart flip-flopped in his chest, and he had to hold back from kissing her. Not yet. Not until she was his again—for good this time. "You've done everything you can *not* to fall in love, Susannah. You did it for good reasons, just as, I suppose, I did, too. You were taking care of your sister. Running a business. Saving for a new life. You had no time, no room, no patience. Pick your reason. I've got a whole briefcase full of them back in New York."

She shook her head, denying it all, but the denial weakened with each shake.

"Why, Susannah?"

The limo rounded another corner, smoothly navigating the streets of Chapel Ridge. Along the sidewalks, everyone stared at the unfamiliar fancy car. Susannah toyed with the frame of the window for a long moment. "When my parents died, the family told me to send Jackie away. To let her live with an aunt in Arizona, so I could have my life. But I couldn't do that."

"Because you loved her too much."

Susannah shifted on the seat, back to Kane. She closed her eyes and sucked in a breath, then shook her head. "Because I had to hold on to what I had left, Kane. And Jackie was all I had."

A single tear slipped down her cheek, and for the first time, Kane noticed the well of emotion in her eyes, brought on by the tumultuous day. One that hadn't just changed Jackie's life, but had made a major shift in Susannah's, too. All those years of watching out for her younger sister, and now the burden was lifted, but he could see, in the pain in her eyes, that a part of her already missed the little bit of family that she'd held on to so tightly.

Kane wrapped an arm around her and drew Susannah to his chest, folding her lithe frame into his. "You did the right thing. It was the most selfless thing anyone could do."

"Don't you understand?" She looked up at him, her cheek against his chest. "I did it for *me*, Kane. Because I couldn't lose her. My parents were dead. My whole world was gone in one day, and if Jackie was gone, too…" She swiped at her face, clearing away newly fallen tears. "It would have been too hard."

She'd been controlling her world, then and now. Boy, did he recognize that trait. He'd inherited more than his height and his eye color from his father. "I do the same thing," Kane said. "Except I devoted myself to my job. I said it was because the company needed me, because my father demanded it, but really, that's an excuse. If I really wanted to find the perfect woman and fall in love, I could have—" a smile crossed his lips "—taken a vacation and done just that."

Slowly, a reciprocal smile curved across her face, and hope took flight in Kane's chest. "Have you taken many of those? Vacations to meet the perfect woman?"

He slid a finger down her delicate nose, landing on her upper lip. The urge to kiss her roared in his chest, thundered in his head. "Only one. Seems the best women are in Chapel Ridge, Indiana."

"Oooh, Mr. Maxwell isn't going to like hearing you say that about his wife."

Kane laughed, then bent down and kissed Susannah after all, bringing her tight to his body, holding her there even after his lips left hers. "I mean you, silly, in case you had any doubts."

She smiled. "I did have some. But they're starting to go away now." She bit her lip, then met his gaze. "You were right, Kane. Maybe I am running from love. It's just… easier when I can hold on to the reins, you know what I mean? When you fall in love, you have to let someone else have one of the reins. And that thought scares the heck out of me."

"I know exactly what you mean." He brushed the hair off her forehead and traced a line down her cheeks, then pressed a kiss along the same path. "And I was wrong to offer you what I did earlier. I was doing exactly what my father always did to me. Controlling everything, because I couldn't stand to lose you. I've realized it's easier to let you go…and open my heart."

"And take a risk?"

He nodded. "It's like having a rough diamond and deciding to cut and polish it while you're blindfolded. You could ruin it, or make it into the most beautiful marquis cut ever. You just have to trust in the stone, and your gut instincts. And my gut says that you and I together will make beautiful gems."

She smiled. "Rubies and emeralds?"

"I don't care if we end up with quartz and topaz. As long as we're together. And hey, we figured out how to fish and light a fire. I'd say after that, this getting married thing will be a piece of cake, what do you say?"

She tipped her head to smile up at him, then a second later, sat up straight, as if the words had just hit her. "Getting married? What do you mean? We just left the wedding."

Kane leaned forward and depressed the button, lowering the window separating them from the driver. "Sam, would you mind heading back to the church?"

"Certainly, Mr. Lennox."

The window went back up, and the limo did a quick U-turn.

"Kane…where are we going?"

Kane slid off the seat and onto the carpeted floor of the limousine. When he had decided that he wanted Susannah, he had moved heaven and earth to make it happen. Having the ring couriered to him, the limo set up, even asking the minister if he had time later today, assuming Susannah might say yes.

Over the years, Kane's billions of dollars had been a frustration in his life, but now he had found that it could also bring him great joy, between the people he had helped, and this.

Kane reached into his jacket pocket and pulled out a flawless two-carat red diamond ring, flanked by four same-sized white diamonds, forming a brilliant floral shape, which caught the sun and cast a rainbow of sparkles around the car. "Susannah Wilson, will you marry me?"

She gaped at the ring, then at him. "Are you crazy? I can't get married. I'm leaving for Paris in the morning and I live here and you live there and—"

He pressed a finger to her lips. "And we'll figure it all out. I always wanted to see Paris as a tourist. But we have to wait, just a few days before we leave for Paris, if that's okay."

"We do? Why?" The words came out in a little stutter, as she took in the ring, him, trying to make sense of it all.

"I promised my father a fishing trip. And believe me, by the time we get back from the church and Jackie's reception, he'll be ready to get out of the house."

She stared at him, confused. "Why?"

"I left him with the same things you gave me. A bag of dog food, a leash and a stray." Kane grinned.

Susannah laughed. "You're trying to convert the whole world?"

"No, just my corner of it." He held out the ring, his heart caught in her eyes, her answer. Never before had so much weighed on one word. "You didn't answer my question. I love you, Susannah. Will you marry me?"

"But where will we live? What will we—"

"Anything is possible."

Susannah looked into Kane's deep blue eyes, and saw the love there, a love she couldn't have believed would happen in such a short time, and felt the same emotion swell in her own heart, and knew he was right. Anything was possible. She'd met a stranger barefoot on her sister's lawn, a stranger with a secret who had forced her to get honest with herself—and had fallen in love with the man he really was.

"Yes," Susannah whispered, as he slid the ring onto her finger. "I love you, Kane."

He took Susannah into his arms and kissed her for a long, long time, loving her sweet goodness, the woman that she was, and the person she had helped him become. Then, when he finally drew back, Kane reached into his pocket and pulled out a small round globe, the kind purchased in airports and tourist shops for desks and curio cabinets.

Nothing special, nothing expensive, but to Susannah, it symbolized the heart of everything she was about. "An early wedding present," he said, pressing it into her palm and curling her hand around the colored globe. "I'll give you the world, if you let me," he said.

Susannah snuggled deeper into Kane's embrace, hearing the steady thump-thump of his heart. "I already have it, right here."

"So do I, Susannah," Kane whispered, "so do I."

CELEBRATE
60 YEARS
OF PURE READING PLEASURE
WITH HARLEQUIN®!

We'll be spotlighting a different series
every month throughout 2009
to celebrate our 60th anniversary.

Look for Harlequin® Blaze™ in March!

O-60

*After all, a lot can happen in 60 years,
or 60 minutes...or 60 seconds!*

Find out what's going down in Blaze's
heart-stopping new miniseries *0-60!*
Getting from "Hello" to "How was it?"
can happen fast....

Look for the brand-new 0-60 miniseries in March 2009!

www.eHarlequin.com   HBRIDE09

HARLEQUIN® Romance®

This February the Harlequin® Romance series
will feature six Diamond Brides stories featuring
diamond proposals and gorgeous grooms.

Share your dream wedding proposal and you could WIN!

The most romantic entry will win a diamond
necklace and will inspire a proposal in one of
our upcoming Diamond Grooms books in 2010.

In 100 words or less, tell us the most romantic
way that you dream of being proposed to.

For more information, and to enter
the Diamond Brides Proposal contest, please visit
www.DiamondBridesProposal.com

Or mail your entry to us at:

IN THE U.S.: 3010 Walden Ave., P.O. Box 9069, Buffalo, NY 14269-9069
IN CANADA: 225 Duncan Mill Road, Don Mills, ON M3B 3K9

No purchase necessary. Contest opens at 12:01 p.m. (ET) on January 15, 2009 and closes at 11:59 p.m.
(ET) on March 13, 2009. One (1) prize will be awarded consisting of a diamond necklace and an author's
fictional adaptation of the contest winner's dream proposal scenario published in an upcoming Harlequin®
Romance novel in February 2010. Approximate retail value of the prize is three thousand dollars ($3000.00
USD). Limit one (1) entry per person per household. Contest open to legal residents of the U.S. (excluding
Colorado) and Canada (excluding Quebec) who have reached the age of majority at time of entry. Void
where prohibited by law. Official Rules available online at www.DiamondBridesProposal.com. Sponsor:
Harlequin Enterprises Limited.

Harlequin® Historical
Historical Romantic Adventure!

The Aikenhead Honours

HIS CAVALRY LADY
Joanna Maitland

Dominic Aikenhead, spy against
the Russians, takes a young soldier
under his wing. "Alex" is actually
Alexandra, a cavalry maiden who
also has been tasked to spy on the
Russians. When Alexandra unveils
herself as a lady, will Dominic flee,
or embrace the woman he has
come to love?

Available March 2009
wherever books are sold.

www.eHarlequin.com   HH29536

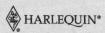
HARLEQUIN®

INTRIGUE®

SPECIAL OPS
TEXAS
COWBOY COMMANDO

BY JOANNA WAYNE

When Linney Kingston's best friend dies in
a drowning accident one day after she told
Linney she was leaving her abusive husband,
Linney is convinced the husband killed her. Linney
goes to the one man she knows can help her, an
ex lover who she's never been able to forget—
Navy SEAL Cutter Martin. They will have to
work together to solve the mystery, but can
they leave their past behind them?

Available March 2009 wherever you buy books.

www.eHarlequin.com

HI69390

Silhouette® *Desire*

BRENDA JACKSON

TALL, DARK... WESTMORELAND!

Olivia Jeffries got a taste of the wild and reckless when she met a handsome stranger at a masquerade ball. In the morning she discovered her new lover was Reginald Westmoreland, her father's most-hated rival. Now Reggie will stop at nothing to get Olivia back in his bed.

**Available March 2009
wherever books are sold.**

Always Powerful, Passionate and Provocative.

www.eHarlequin.com

SD76928

REQUEST YOUR FREE BOOKS!
2 FREE NOVELS PLUS 2
FREE GIFTS!

HARLEQUIN ROMANCE®

From the Heart, For the Heart

YES! Please send me 2 FREE Harlequin Romance® novels and my 2 FREE gifts (gifts are worth about $10). After receiving them, if I don't wish to receive any more books, I can return the shipping statement marked "cancel". If I don't cancel, I will receive 4 brand-new novels every month and be billed just $3.32 per book in the U.S. or $3.80 per book in Canada, plus 25¢ shipping and handling per book and applicable taxes, if any*. That's a savings of over 15% off the cover price! I understand that accepting the 2 free books and gifts places me under no obligation to buy anything. I can always return a shipment and cancel at any time. Even if I never buy another book, the two free books and gifts are mine to keep forever.

114 HDN ERQW   314 HDN ERQ9

Name	(PLEASE PRINT)	
Address		Apt. #
City	State/Prov.	Zip/Postal Code

Signature (if under 18, a parent or guardian must sign)

Mail to the **Harlequin Reader Service:**
IN U.S.A.: P.O. Box 1867, Buffalo, NY 14240-1867
IN CANADA: P.O. Box 609, Fort Erie, Ontario L2A 5X3

Not valid to current subscribers of Harlequin Romance books.

Want to try two free books from another line?
Call 1-800-873-8635 or visit www.morefreebooks.com.

* Terms and prices subject to change without notice. N.Y. residents add applicable sales tax. Canadian residents will be charged applicable provincial taxes and GST. Offer not valid in Quebec. This offer is limited to one order per household. All orders subject to approval. Credit or debit balances in a customer's account(s) may be offset by any other outstanding balance owed by or to the customer. Please allow 4 to 6 weeks for delivery. Offer available while quantities last.

Your Privacy: Harlequin Books is committed to protecting your privacy. Our Privacy Policy is available online at www.eHarlequin.com or upon request from the Reader Service. From time to time we make our lists of customers available to reputable third parties who may have a product or service of interest to you. If you would prefer we not share your name and address, please check here. ☐

HR08R

You're invited to join our Tell Harlequin Reader Panel!

By joining our new reader panel you will:

- Receive Harlequin® books—they are FREE and yours to keep with no obligation to purchase anything!
- Participate in fun online surveys
- Exchange opinions and ideas with women just like you
- Have a say in our new book ideas and help us publish the best in women's fiction

In addition, you will have a chance to win great prizes and receive special gifts! See Web site for details. Some conditions apply. Space is limited.

To join, visit us at
www.TellHarlequin.com.

Coming Next Month

Available March 10, 2009

**Spring is here and romance is in the air this month
as Harlequin Romance® takes you on a whirlwind journey
to meet gorgeous grooms!**

#4081 BRADY: THE REBEL RANCHER Patricia Thayer
Second in the **Texas Brotherhood** duet. Injured pilot Brady falls for the
lovely Lindsey Stafford, but she has secrets that could destroy him. Now
Brady must fight again, this time for love....

#4082 ITALIAN GROOM, PRINCESS BRIDE Rebecca Winters
We visit the **Royal House of Savoy** as Princess Regina's arranged
wedding day approaches. Royal gardener Dizo has one chance to risk
all—and claim his princess bride!

#4083 FALLING FOR HER CONVENIENT HUSBAND Jessica Steele
Successful lawyer Phelix isn't the same shy teenager Nathan
conveniently wed eight years ago. He hasn't seen her since, and her
transformation hasn't escaped the English tycoon's notice....

#4084 CINDERELLA'S WEDDING WISH Jessica Hart
In Her Shoes...
Celebrity playboy Rafe is *not* Miranda's idea of Prince Charming. But
when she's hired as his assistant, Miranda is shocked to learn that Rafe
has hidden depths.

#4085 HER CATTLEMAN BOSS Barbara Hannay
When Kate inherits half a run-down cattle station, she doesn't expect to
have a sexy cattleman boss, Noah, to contend with! As they toil under
the hot sun, romance is on the horizon....

#4086 THE ARISTOCRAT AND THE SINGLE MOM Michelle Douglas
Handsome English aristocrat Simon keeps to himself. But, thrown into
the middle of single mom Kate's lively family on a trip to Australia, Simon
finds his buttoned-up manner slowly undone.